"Aaron, do   " Y
asked hopefully.

"Pretty? You're delicious," he told her, his hands caressing her naked shoulders. He licked a finger and brush stroked the tender skin of her throat. "Let's see if you taste as good as you look."

Her body sang and her heart cried out, for even as he wooed her, he was denying her the right to truly be his wife. "Love me, Aaron," she begged him, then demanded, "*Love me.*"

"No," he groaned, then pulled her tighter against him, unwilling to give in or give her up.

Addy vowed to herself that she wasn't giving up until his half-hearted no was a resounding yes. She kissed him back with everything she had, until he rolled away and knelt beside her.

"You don't want me to love you," he told her. "If I do, I'll devour you. Obsession is a dangerous thing, Addy, and that's what this would be. We could kill each other, me suffocating you with my needs, while you clawed me to death trying to breathe free. You don't want me to love you, because if I did, I'd need you even more than I do now."

"I need you," she cried. "I don't understand what this feeling is, but it's killing me alive."

Aaron groaned, then pulled her into his arms. "Say your prayers, babydoll. I'm past ready to make you die with pleasure. . . ."

WHAT ARE *LOVESWEPT* ROMANCES?

They are stories of true romance and touching emotion. We believe those two very important ingredients are constants in our highly sensual and very believable stories in the LOVESWEPT line. Our goal is to give you, the reader, stories of consistently high quality that may sometimes make you laugh, sometimes make you cry, but are always fresh and creative and contain many delightful surprises within their pages.

Most romance fans read an enormous number of books. Those they truly love, they keep. Others may be traded with friends and soon forgotten. We hope that each LOVESWEPT romance will be a treasure—a "keeper." We will always try to publish

LOVE STORIES YOU'LL NEVER FORGET
BY AUTHORS YOU'LL ALWAYS REMEMBER

The Editors

SHOTGUN WEDDING

OLIVIA RUPPRECHT

BANTAM BOOKS
NEW YORK · TORONTO · LONDON · SYDNEY · AUCKLAND

SHOTGUN WEDDING

A Bantam Book / April 1994

*If you would be interested in receiving protective vinyl covers for your
Loveswept books, please write to this address for information:*

> Loveswept
> Bantam Books
> P.O. Box 985
> Hicksville, NY 11802

ISBN 0-553-44307-0

Published simultaneously in the United States and Canada

Bantam Books are published by Bantam Books, a division of Bantam Doubleday Dell Publishing Group, Inc. Its trademark, consisting of the words
"Bantam Books" and the portrayal of a rooster, is Registered in U.S. Patent
and Trademark Office and in other countries. Marca Registrada. Bantam
Books, 1540 Broadway, New York, New York 10036.

PRINTED IN THE UNITED STATES OF AMERICA

OPM   0 9 8 7 6 5 4 3 2 1

For Daddy

Who took me in search of rainbow's end,
and taught me that the pot of gold is
never beyond reach,
that the best riches are found along life's way
as we pursue our dreams.

The only real failure is the fear to try.

PROLOGUE

"I thank you for the books, Aaron. But I thank you even more for the fancy new dress. Like it?" Addy sashayed into the small barn, fresh hay crunching beneath her scuffed black boots. Several twigs caught in the sole, which was coming apart from the shoe leather.

She should have looked silly, or even a little pitiful, in those awful worn-out boots and the simple cotton sundress he'd brought from New York to Half-moon Hollow. God's country, or so hamlet dwellers called it. But to an outsider, even a self-made one like himself, this hidden pocket of Appalachia was closer to the vision striding toward him in a sad pair of shoes: gorgeous scenery wrapped in poverty and pride.

No, Addy didn't look silly or pitiful by a long shot, and at the moment Aaron wished that she did.

Where had the little girl gone? Only the flowing, wild mane of her sable hair marked her as the child he'd always harbored a special fondness for. It amazed him how much she'd matured since his last visit two years ago, when she'd been a coltish twelve-year-old. That was the girl he'd bought the dress for, not this woman-child with a lush, feminine body.

Aaron was suddenly sorry he'd given her the secret gift earlier that day. Especially now that it was night and the tight binding of the dress enhanced her graceful movements as she slowly moved closer.

She twirled, and the skirt flirted around long bare legs.

"So? Like what you see?"

"It's . . ." *Riveting. Risqué. Two sizes too small and totally inappropriate*. Lord, if any of the local boys saw her in the thing, they'd be after her like a pack of rutting dogs. Not even he, ever the doting mentor of sorts, was immune.

Something instinctive and disturbing stirred inside him. He was tempted to tell Addy to head home and never dare put that dress on again. But she looked so expectant and hopeful, so obviously wanted his approval, that he couldn't bring himself to hurt her feelings.

"The dress looks nice on you, Addy."

"I'm awfully glad you think so." She gave him a beaming smile, then glanced down to admire the bodice. Aaron realized that he was admiring her bodice too. "It *is* nice, isn't it?"

Nice? About as nice as the shocking jolt of his masculine reaction. Proof positive that he'd gotten what he came for—absorbing his heritage, which was destined for canvas and clay in a SoHo loft. *Some heritage*, he thought as Addy strolled closer, a birthplace where his attraction to a much younger distant relation wasn't way out of line.

Her waist-length hair, dark as a moonless night, swayed in time with her hips. She had a walk that was aloof and sultry, a poised glide that was somehow straightforward and cocky at once. It suited her. As for the arousal it incited, that didn't suit Aaron one little bit.

He busied himself by lighting another lantern, then looked at her with a stern gaze.

"You shouldn't be here, Addy. You're already in trouble for sneaking over to see me during the day. If your folks knew you'd traipsed through the pass to hunt down a Breedlove this late at night, they'd be upset. *Real* upset."

"Oh, they'd have hissy fits for a fact, likely give me enough chores to last me to old age. But what they don't know won't hurt 'em—and unless you tell on me, I should be safe."

Safe was not what he was feeling at the moment. The barn belonging to his father was small, considering that Judson Breedlove was the reigning clansman on this side of the hamlet. But the closer Addy came, the smaller the space seemed. By the time she walked two work-roughened fingers up his chest, there was barely room left to breathe.

Aaron inhaled sharply. The smell of fresh rainwater and wildflowers stirred his senses to a dangerous level, and though his instincts urged him to touch her sweet-smelling hair, morals demanded he put an end to this quick.

He caught her wrist. The innocent contact didn't feel innocent. It was laced with a current of sexual heat that defied age differences and an outside society's disapproval. It wasn't right for him to be feeling these things. It wasn't right for Addy to be teasing him like this. But then again, she was only a simple mountain girl trying out her feminine charms on a man of the world and had no idea she might be courting disaster.

"You're playing with fire," he warned softly. "Careful, Addy, or you could get burned."

She answered him by licking her finger, pressing it to his lips, and softly hissing, "*Sssss.*"

He couldn't have said it better himself. As he stared down at her, the blush of her cheeks reminding him of small apples ripened by the sun, her bluer than blue eyes sparked with mischief and intimate invitation, he steeled himself to meet her challenge.

"You know, Addy, when I bought that dress, I had no idea you'd grown into such a tempting young woman."

"What if I hadn't showed? Would you've given this pretty thing to your sister instead, or come hunting me down?"

"I knew you'd find me when no one was looking. After all, we've always been special to each other. Me, telling you stories about the big city. You, singing me those songs you make up while I'm gone. And I do have to say I'm amazed by just how much you've grown since my last visit."

Slowly lowering his gaze, drawn by the alluring sight of her breasts filling out the white cotton bodice, he suddenly questioned what he was planning to do. But Addy was so special, so different from both their kin, and he wanted better for her than where she was recklessly heading.

Holding to his purpose, he gripped a fistful of hair at her nape and angled her face to his.

"Have you ever been kissed?" he roughly demanded.

"No," she answered on a throaty sigh, much too seductive and filled with an innocent yearning that caught at him, twisted him up in places he struggled to ignore. "Lots of boys have tried, mind you. But I was waiting." She licked lush lips that were provocative by nature and didn't need lipstick, even if she'd had some.

"I was waiting for you, Aaron. Every night I dream about you, about us. And I sleep with that doll you brung—I mean, brought—me. See? I'm even talking different since I've been studying those books you gave me. I wanted to make you proud, prove I could learn to be like you."

"Take my word for it, you don't want to be like me." Knowing just how humanly flawed he was made him feel both wonderful and unworthy when she continued to look up at him as if he were some god in the sky. "Be yourself and make us both proud by staying out of trouble. Coming here like this, coming on to me, it's not smart." He gave her a shake that sent her hair tumbling over his hands, which were themselves trembling.

"I'm twenty-five, little girl, not sixteen. Consider yourself lucky that I've still got some scruples and a lot more sense than you do. You'd better wise up, Addy, before you get yourself in trouble with some boy who doesn't have a lick of ambition or the inclination to turn away what you came here offering. Do I make myself clear?"

She pressed her palm against his chest and stroked. "What's clear to me is that your heart's beating like a rainstorm on a tin roof. Maybe you've made yourself into an outsider, but your papa's blood runs true in your veins. When he was the chosen son, he picked your mama from all the other McDonald women, and she was scarce a year older than me. Look at me, Aaron, look at me good, and tell if what you see is a little girl. Or do you see a woman old enough to bear children, tend a house, and work the land? I loved you when I was a child, but now I'm a woman. *In love*. With you."

"You don't know what you're saying or doing." He'd meant to say it kindly, but his words emerged sharp, directed more to himself than her. "You'd better leave," he said gruffly. "Go on now, before you make this situation worse than it is."

"But I *do* love you," she declared passionately, tugging at his shirt. "And I want you something fierce!"

"Damn, enough already!" As he thrust away her hand, Aaron damned himself for the hunger she provoked, the temptation of grabbing her back to crush her mouth with his. Shunning his forbidden lust, he snapped, "You don't love me. You *can't*. Baby, you don't even know me."

"That's not true, not true at all. Why, I know you better'n anyone in the hollow. You're kind and sweet and—"

"Try temperamental, with an emphasis on *temper*. Be smart and go home. If you don't, you're going to find out that I can be anything but kind and sweet." He pointed an unsteady finger at the barn door she'd closed on her way in. "Make tracks like white lightnin', and don't you *ever* wiggle your tail under my nose again, or I'll tan your hide before your papa can. You deaf, girl? I *said*, git!"

His words rebounded with a mocking echo in his head. Eight years he'd spent refining himself, carving his niche in the art world by virtue of the same roots he was desperate to put behind him. Now, thanks to Addy, the old roots were tangling around his feet, making him fear he would stumble and fall. On Addy. Fall on her as if she truly were a woman, not one in the making whose perspective was shaded by this secluded, closed society.

She leveled him with an in-your-face stare while slowly dropping to her knees. Hands raised in supplication, she held his gaze captive with hers, demanding he confront all that she was. Her pride. Maturity. A sensuality of stark beauty.

But it was the willful streak, a gritty determination to rival his own, that commanded his grudging respect.

"You don't have to love me back, Aaron, 'cause I love you enough for us both. Take me with you. *Please*. Take me away from here to that world where you go. I won't be any trouble, I promise. I'll cook your meals, clean your house, mend your clothes. And if you don't want to bed me till you decide just maybe you love me some, too, that's something I won't fight—"

"No." His terse refusal coincided with an inner wince of empathy. Their blood ties were distant, but they were woven tight in their mutual thirst for more. More than this impoverished, rich land and the century-old feud that tied the McDonalds to the Breedloves like a shared umbilical cord. He felt for Addy, deeply. And though he'd tried, it just wasn't in him to turn her away so meanly.

"Look, I'm sorry," he told her. "Because I know how you feel—so trapped, you think you'll go crazy before finding a way to get out. But I'm not your way out, Addy McDonald. I *can't* be, no matter how much I wish I could give that to you."

"But anything you wish, you can make happen. You can do anything, Aaron. Why, every soul in the hills with half a brain knows it. Just look at the way you ran off, with your papa screaming at your back, and when you came home it was in your very own airplane! And you had on those fancy clothes and brought all sorts of fancy stuff from the outside and—"

"Addy, get up." When he tried to lift her, her skin beneath his palms felt like hot clay, pliable and earthy. Dear God, what had he ever done to deserve this? How could he endure the grasp of her arms around his legs, her cheek pressed against his upper thigh while she thanked him again and again for the books, the magazines with the glossy ads . . . ?

"And, Aaron, oh, Aaron, the places I go in my mind. With you, always with you. I close my eyes, and we're together on a ship, or barefoot on sand so white, it hurts to look at, or—or sometimes I see us in a room so fine, I can't believe a body could ever bear to go outside. Don't leave me here," she pleaded. "We can steal away. Tonight, we could run off and—"

"And our families would have a whole new quarrel with each other. It's not an easy truce as it is, you know that. And I'm not about to give my father more grief than I already have." Stroking her head, he offered what comfort and understanding he could as he proceeded to shatter her dreams.

"Besides, where I live now, a grown man can't take in an underage girl without the authorities wanting some answers. And even if they didn't, I have a career that doesn't leave room for you. I know that sounds cruel, but that's just the way it is. Try to understand. Even if you can't, you'll just have to take my 'no' as final."

"I understand just fine." She got to her feet, knuckling tears from her cheeks as she did. "Those are good reasons all right, reasons wrapped in lies. Ashamed of where you come from and us livin' here, that's what you are. Got yourself a shiny new life, Aaron Breedlove, and you don't want some backwoods kin reminding you of what you are inside . . . or sheddin' light on what you hide from other eyes."

Addy raised her chin, daring him to argue the truth. There was an unmistakable triumph in her fierce gaze. In that moment Aaron thought her the most ravishing sight he'd ever beheld: Addy, glorious in her fury at the man who had refused her an escape. Thank God she'd yet to come into her own because as it was he felt bested by a child.

"Congratulations," he said quietly. "Maybe you do know me. Got me where it hurts. Funny, how humans take such a perverse pleasure in hurting those we profess to love."

Her brow arched, and she let go a short, brittle laugh. "Seems I waited all this time for a man who's scared of a hillbilly girl. Never mind the kiss, I'll get my first from any boy I pick . . . and soon. Real soon. While you're flying in the sky, think of me bein' with someone else, and just you remember it could've been you." She turned to walk away.

Before he could think past his need to have the last word, Aaron caught the flyaway whip of her hair with one hand while his other spun her around by the waist.

"Not so fast, girl. You want a kiss? Well, I do too." Aaron stroked her arms with a calculated gentleness, then gripped them hard, his fingertips exerting a biting pressure. Oh yes, there was a price attached to provocation, and that was something Addy was about to learn. Breathing in her soft gasp, he said in a hot whisper, "A *bad* kiss, baby. The badder, the better. That's how I like it." He couldn't believe his own words, but he didn't know any other way to get his message across.

Intent on scaring some sense into her, he pressed a hand to Addy's throat and felt for her pulse. *Thump, thump, thump.* Good. Her heart was beating like crazy.

So was his.

"Me, scared of a hillbilly girl?" he murmured. "We'll see who's scared by the time I'm through with you."

"Make me scared? Of what, pray tell?" Addy retorted. "Of gettin' kissed, gettin' bred, and living out my hand-to-mouth days in a shack as poor as the one where I'm already living?"

Even as she said it, Addy's heart sank. The picture she'd painted was too familiar for comfort, a life she craved to escape. *With Aaron.* Aaron, who had gotten free of this prison whose bars were mountains and traditions etched in time. Aaron, her only love for now and forever. She had to make him understand they belonged together, just like in the storybooks he'd brought her. With each turn of the page she saw him, her knight in shining armor sweeping up his damsel in distress to ride into the sunset and live happily ever after.

Only . . . that growling noise he was making wasn't quite right. Aaron sounded more like the Big Bad Wolf than Prince Charming come to claim her with a sweet kiss.

"Well, what're you waiting for?" Addy prayed the tremor inside her didn't tell in her voice. His eyes seemed to be devouring her, all hungry and hot. But the Beast had no doubt looked at Beauty that way—and she always had loved the Beast.

Aaron began walking her backward. As he tilted her back, Addy gripped his shirt to steady her balance. The feel of the cloth was so fine, so smooth and crisp, and the feel of Aaron's skin beneath it so marvelous, it stole her breath.

What breath she had left was nearly knocked out of her when he pushed her roughly onto a pile of hay. He towered over her, big as Goliath, legs spread over her own. Aaron wasn't acting at all like himself. The Aaron she knew would never hurt her—except for the pain he'd brought to her heart. And he'd felt bad for that.

He had to be up to something—and that something was so obvious that what fear she'd felt vanished. *Aaron was trying to scare her away*. Addy decided then and there that he was going to find out he'd met his match.

His perfect match, to be exact.

Patting the hay beside her, she said truthfully, "I'm lonesome, Aaron, and there's plenty of room for two. You've always been the best company I've ever kept. Come keep me company?" And then, in a heartfelt whisper: "Come hold me like you'll never let me go."

He hesitated, staring at her and muttering something that sounded between a curse and a prayer. She reached up and grabbed his shirt to pull him down and rent the beautiful fabric, sending those fancy buttons on his shirt flying.

Addy couldn't endure such waste. She scrambled for the nearest one. *Lord, but it must be a pearl!* Claiming it between the smooth leather of his shoes, she felt his hand clamp down hard on hers.

"You want my button, Addy?"

"More than anything . . . except for you."

Oh, Addy, she thought she heard him whisper before he growled, "Oh yeah? Better learn to be careful for what you ask. You're liable to get more than what you bargained for."

He dropped to his knees and pried open her hand to take back his throwaway prize. And then she felt the glide of his finger, pushing the button down her dress between her breasts. She felt as if Aaron himself was touching her there.

In thanks she threw her arms around him, and the wondrous pleasure of his nearness made her beg for a tighter hug. There was some scent on him that she'd never been able to get close enough to. And even now, the closest she'd ever got, with her nose buried in the crook of his neck, it was still a kind of tease. Tasting it, she took a lick. Then another and another, until she was bathing his neck with her tongue.

"Dear God, Addy, what are you doing?" His groan made her wonder if he was in some sort of pain.

If it matched the pain she was feeling, then Aaron was near to death. The ache deep in her belly was coiled up like a rattler ready to strike, just like the rattler he'd saved her from when she was barely six. She could still remember the strength of those arms, the security she felt as he held her. And now, here they were holding her even closer, only not close enough to appease this painful, wonderful longing. She arched up to get as close to him as she could.

"Addy." His whisper brushed her neck. So did his lips.

"Aaron," she whispered back, pressing her lips to him in similar fashion. Heeding her instincts, she wrapped her thighs around his—only for Aaron to quit hugging her and try to pry her legs loose.

Ignoring his efforts, she touched his face, his shoulders, marveling that his powerful strength could make her feel so weak with yearning. His hair, the color of corn silk and just as fine, gave way to her feathering of thick lashes over pale blue eyes. The slope of those majestic shoulders tensed as she stroked the lean muscles of his back. When she reached lower, he gave up on unlatching her legs and battled her for possession of her searching hands.

He was the finest man ever to walk the earth, and he felt so incredibly good that she wasn't about to let him go.

"Addy," he bit out, then sucked in a great gulp of air, " . . . let go of me. Do it . . . now. *Now!*" Frantic to keep him, she held on even tighter so that Aaron had to all but throw her off. Before her back hit the hay, he was moving away with a desperate speed. Palms spread against the barn's planking, she watched his head fall forward between his shoulders. Broad, manly shoulders she ached to touch.

Even more she ached to run to him, wrap her arms around him, and tell him again and again that she loved him more than ever. But something about the shaking of his head, the stiffness of his spine, said he wanted none of that.

"Aaron?" She spoke his name softly, caressing it around her tongue.

"Go home, Addy," he whispered. Then his fist smacked the wood, and he barked, "Go! Go home and . . . and we'll pretend none of this ever happened."

"Never happened!" she protested, his words lashing at her worse than a stinging slap. "Of course it happened—and it was wonderful and don't you dare try taking it back!" His silence hurt more than what he'd said. He was sending her away, acting as if she didn't exist. Before she could stop herself, she hurled a fistful of dried dung at his back. He flinched, but still he wouldn't look at her.

Desperate for some acknowledgment, she screamed at him, "I'm talking to you, Aaron Breedlove, and when I speak to you, you are to look at me! I am a person. I am a woman. And you will treat me with respect. Turn around and *look* at me."

Slowly, he turned. Even more slowly, he said, "If you were a woman, you'd realize that respect is exactly what I'm trying to show . . . little girl."

How anyone could hurt this much and still live, she didn't know. Her only comfort was in realizing she wasn't alone. Never in her life had she seen a look such as the one on Aaron's face. Shock. Defeat. All mixed with a seething hunger that was dark and deep. And ashamed.

He was ashamed for touching her, for wanting her, that message was clear. His gaze was like a touch, a searing touch that torched the distance he'd put between them.

He wanted her as much as she did him, that was plain. But Aaron didn't love her back the way she loved him, and Addy suddenly hated him a little for that.

She rose and went to him, determined to make him admit what he was denying. But when she laid her cheek against his back and reached to hug his waist, he bellowed, "That does it!" In a flash he had her pushed against the barn wall. In a lethal whisper he said, "I'm giving you to the count of ten to march your butt home. If I have to do it for you, I'll be telling your folks exactly what you've been up to."

About the only thing she had left inside her was pride. And her pride demanded that she not leave on a threat.

"You want me," she stated, matter-of-fact.

"The hell I do, you little she-cat. You're an accident just waiting to happen and it's not about to happen with me. Read my lips, Addy: *I . . . do . . . not . . . want . . . you. One. Two. Three—*"

"That's a lie. I can see it in your eyes, feel it in your body." A lick of his white knuckles braced above her shoulder, and she whispered, "I can even taste it on your skin. You want me, Aaron. Don't try to deny it."

Deciding she'd better leave before she gave in to the buckets of tears she was close to crying, Addy ducked under his braced arm and marched regally to the barn door.

Once there, she turned.

"By the way, you never did give me my first kiss." After blowing him one, she pulled open the door and slipped into the moonless night.

Aaron stared at the empty doorway long after she was gone, and he heard her wrenching sobs long after they ceased to carry over the wind.

What had Addy done to him? Whatever it was, it left him feeling disoriented, like a confused boy who had very nearly been seduced.

Aaron wondered when he'd stop wishing that Addy had succeeded. One thing was certain:

He wouldn't be back until that wish went away.

ONE

"I'll be a'waitin', waitin' for him . . . For that man who broke my heart on a whim. . . ." Addy squeezed the cow's udder in time to the song. Making up the words as she went, she tasted the flavor of emotion, felt the rhythm echo her heartbeat. "His touch, it was so gentle, so rough. . . . And now I'm cryin' 'cause it wasn't enough. . . . No, never enou—"

"Addy! Addy, he's here! Sure as shootin' and plain as day, he's here! Saw him with my own two eyes, and may God strike me dead if I'm lyin'!"

Peering around the cow she was milking, Addy watched her sister rush into the stall at a dead run, stopping just short of a cow patty. But her mouth kept on going.

"Mercy, Loretta, you're babbling faster than a flooded brook and not making a lick of sense. Sit down and catch your breath while I finish my chores."

"Are you tellin' me that you're going to shovel cow dung while the man you've been pining for day and night for four years is almost within spittin' distance and—"

"*What!*" Addy jumped up so fast, she upended the pail of milk destined for dinner and their family of ten. Breathless, she whispered, "Aaron," then shouted, "Aaron!" Grabbing Loretta, she whirled her around twice, then stopped in midtwirl. "It *is* Aaron?" she demanded. "You're not playing a mean joke on me for hiding your clothes when I caught you and Whit skinny-dipping the other night?"

"I was mad, but I would never pay you back so cruel. I know what he means to you—though Lord only knows why. Wastin' your life away and all for a man that might as well be living on the moon. But he's there on the other side of the mountain. Puts him about as close as the stars, his being a Breedlove and all."

"Last names never did mean a hill of beans between Aaron and me."

"Maybe not a hill of beans, but the mountain between his and ours counts for plenty."

Wrinkling her nose at that, Addy felt for the necklace made of embroidery thread and tightly grasped the cherished button she wore as a pendant. One touch and she was reliving that glorious, bittersweet night when he'd spoiled her for any other man. Aaron, strong, refined, and worldly—the memory of him still made her blood hum. Praise be she hadn't settled for less than the man she'd set her sights on.

"Uh-oh," Loretta said. "You wouldn't be plannin' to get into some mischief, would you?"

"Me? Mischief? Why, Loretta, whatever do you mean?"

"Going over there to see him, that's what."

"After he kept me waiting all this time, you don't think I'm about to hunt him down looking like this? It'll take me a while to get spruced up so fine that one glimpse and Aaron will wonder whatever possessed him to leave me behind."

"I thought you was smart, not dumb as a hangnail."

"Of course I'm smart! Smart enough to wait for Aaron when I could've had my pick."

"But if you was his pick, don't you think he would've come after you instead of hightailing it in the opposite direction?"

Addy wanted to yank Loretta's hair for that. And would have if she'd spoken meanly, not with sisterly concern. "Makes sense, far as I can see. He likely got word his pa was sick and, fine man that Aaron is, he was sure to tend to family before personal pleasure. That pleasure being *me*. Don't you know that hearts don't lie? And mine tells me that a woman can't feel so strong for a man without him feeling something too." Addy paused. "Right? After all, we always were special to each other, Aaron said so himself. He was just waiting for me to get a bit older, that's all. Am I right, or am I right?"

Gaze lowered, Loretta mumbled, "Right. But even being right won't change the fact that old man Breedlove's sure to pass anytime. And if it's Jonas he picks to keep the truce, then . . . well, you know."

The heavy silence that fell between them was suddenly broken by the pail banging into the rafters. Addy jiggled her throbbing foot and hitched her hands on her hips.

"I'll tell you what I know." With a desperate passion she declared, "Aaron's back, and I won't take any part in that silly old ritual. Aaron's back, and—"

"And if he *is* here for you, then he'd better take you for a wife quick," Loretta said, her tone firm. "Can't be a Shriner or a Donning or anyone else. You're a McDonald, and a McDonald it has to be. No, Addy, not even you would break tradition after a hundred years of it being law in our lands."

While Addy's mind called that a lie, in her heart she wasn't sure if she could shame her family by refusing to honor the age-old ritual. To defy this, the most revered of all traditions, would make her a traitor to their ways, worse than those who had left the hamlet for the outside. Aaron was a traitor of sorts, but he held a special position she couldn't claim: son of the Breedlove most high.

Son of the Breedlove most high . . .

"Wait a minute . . . if Aaron vows to keep the truce—"

"You're talkin' a miracle, Addy."

"A miracle for sure, but today's a day for miracles." Eyes to heaven, she prayed fiercely, "Oh please, please, God, *let it be him*."

Loretta took Addy's clasped hands and held them tight. "For you, I pray it happens. But, Addy, if he's already married, not even God can change that."

❦ ——————————— ❦

In the hour since he'd arrived home, Aaron had decided it would take an act of God to change his father's way of thinking. Giving up on that, he appealed to his mother.

"Look, my plane's only ten miles away. Once we get Papa there, I can have him in a hospital within two hours and—"

"Hospital," his father croaked from the feather mattress where he struggled to sit up. "Don't you dare take me to some witch doctor, or I'll haunt every one of you till you draw your last breaths." Judson Breedlove still had enough life left to hack out a demand for more garlic and ramps.

The remedy for a sick heart was put into his mouth while the faith healer passed a hand over Judd's stricken chest. Three times she did this to "push away the sickness" while mouthing the secret chant of faith that would be violated should she speak it aloud. The only way Aaron managed to keep his own mouth shut was by reminding himself of the miracles he'd seen the healer work. But when she shook her head as if to say, "No miracles today," he threw up his hands.

"Damn, can't you see that he's dying?" Aaron shouted, as if they were deaf as well as blind. "Jesus, Mama—"

"Don't you go takin' the Lord's name in vain! Do it agin and I'll wash your mouth out with soap, and don't think for a minute I won't."

His own mother, the best ally he had, had just sealed her husband's fate. As for her threat, Aaron didn't doubt she'd make good on it. He might be a full-grown man, strong enough to wrestle a grizzly, but no way was he taking on thirty-odd relations that looked ready to pounce.

What Sue Ellen Breedlove decreed was as good as gospel. And he never had developed a taste for lye soap.

"Okay, have it your way. You and Papa both. No hospital, all right? But just you remember that his blood is on your hands, not mine."

"God's hands, you mean." Preacher Green, an elderly man from the hollow, didn't make any bones about siding with those steeped in the old beliefs. "When it's time, it's time, and that's all there is to it. Where's your respect, boy? Did you leave it on the outside where folks is hooked up on machines and denied the right to die with dignity? It's devilish and wrong and got no place here. Do right and honor your father and mother as the Bible says. Either do it and stay—or leave us be."

Aaron's gaze swept from face to face, all his closest relations silently upholding the ultimatum.

Hard as it was, Aaron knew he had no choice. "Sorry, Mama. Papa, you too. Even if I don't like it, this is your choice, and so be it." He went to his father then and grasped the shaking hand the elderly man held out. How it hurt him to see Papa this way, a ghost of the strapping mountaineer Aaron had loved, defied, and in his life outside the hollow been so ashamed of that he'd denied his existence.

Aaron suddenly felt even guiltier. Kneeling by the bed, he said, "I shouldn't have stayed away so long."

"But you did. Why, Son? Was it those hard words we had the day you left?"

Those hard words had been about Addy. His father had seen her leave the barn and had demanded to know if *his* son had been dallying with *that* girl, who was *the* orneriest, most highhanded, prissiest britches that *any* McDonald had ever spawned. Angered by the way his father had run her down, he'd come to Addy's defense. A shouting match to rival any they'd ever had ended when he stalked away. His father called to him; he didn't look back.

A terrible dry spell had finally sent him here to confront the reason for it. His master dealer was about to disown him; his personal life was on the rocks and sliding. And how much of it was because of Addy?

Putting aside his need to ask for news of her, Aaron said quietly, "I didn't stay away because of you, Papa. I just got caught up with work and demands and—and if I could do it all over again, I'd do better by you than I have."

A lump settled in the back of his throat. It was hard to talk, even harder to say what needed to be said. "We've had more than distance keeping us apart, Papa. There's been a lot of hurt on both sides, but I've hurt you the deepest. I want to put things right if there's any way I can."

"So . . . if I want a promise, then you'll make good on it once I'm gone?" His father's eyes fixed on Sue Ellen; there seemed no doubt as to the promise about to be asked.

"Anything for Mama, anytime."

"Much as I appreciate it, shouldn't be much for you to do . . . got your brothers and sisters here to watch after her."

Murmuring assurances of that, his siblings pressed in closer, then closer still at the sound of a papery wheeze. Aaron could feel their eyes on him, could feel the force of their grief riding an undercurrent of raw anger. Four brothers, two sisters, bearing down on him, resenting the youngest son and rightfully so. He had been the one who deserted the family, the one who put himself above them and the ways of life they held most dear.

Papa's grip slackened, and Aaron felt the full burden of his past slights. He felt an equally dire need to atone before it was too late.

"Name your wish, and it's yours," he vowed earnestly. "Anything you want, Papa. Anything except—"

"You'll agree to anything he wants," boomed a voice that sounded like his uncle Ned's, followed by a shout from one of his cousins.

"That's right! It was you who broke his heart, heard him say so myself. If it's your last breath he's wanting, any son wouldn't think twice about giving it."

A roar of agreement swept the room.

Their outrage, carrying a note of hysteria, caused Aaron's guilt to double while another emotion kicked in: fear. Fear of their anger. Worse still was the fear of that part of himself that understood too well how they thought, how they felt, how justified they were to band against him.

"I love you, Papa," he whispered fervently. And then loud enough for everyone to hear, he said again, "I love you so much that I'd give up my life if it meant you could keep yours. But that's not going to happen, and I have to go on once you're gone. I'm sorry, but the one thing I can't do is come back to Half-moon Hollow to live."

The dry whisper of his father's gentle laugh stilled the less than gentle murmurs rippling the deathbed air.

"Why, Son, that's a wish too selfish for me ever to ask. I'm proud of you." The space of a minute passed while his father struggled for ample strength to go on. "What shames me is folks saying you think yourself above the rest of us. Prove it untrue. That's my dyin' wish."

"Prove it? Any way I can."

His father opened his eyes to reveal a gaze that was sharp and clear. Aaron knew that look: Papa had lured him into a steel trap and, unless he were to gnaw off his foot, he'd been caught.

"Live where you want, boy, but first take the vow and keep the truce . . . that keeps things peaceful. I'll die . . . die happy if you agree."

The vow. The truce. Of all things for his father to ask, he never dreamed it would be to bear the honor of the chosen son. Given the significance of the rite and Papa's condition, it made no sense for him not to have named his successor before now. And *him*, of all sons to choose—

Aaron was suddenly frantic to give back the coveted mantle. He hadn't exactly promised to accept it. *Had he?*

"Papa, I don't know what to say—"

"I know you're grateful, Son. No need for you to thank me."

Judson managed a sly wink. Suddenly, Aaron wasn't sure whether his father was getting even or making amends.

"Of course I'm grateful. And ... touched. More than touched, but—but I'm not worthy. Believe me, *please*, such an honor belongs to a son more deserving and—"

"Oh, you're deserving, Son."

"No, I'm not! Besides, I'm—"

"Married off already, are you?"

"No, but—"

"Taking back your word?"

"No, but I—"

"Know why we could never ... get along? We've always been the spitting image of each other. Death came knockin' yesterday but ... I knew you'd come. So I waited. Waited to hand down what my own papa gave me. I'm tired now and ... Sue Ellen? Lord but I ... always will love—" His head slumped to the side, his father's eyes were frozen in a sightless stare.

"Papa!" Pulling him into his arms, Aaron said in a choked voice, "Papa, Papa, don't die. Not yet, please. I'm sorry for everything, but I—"

"*Judson.*" Claiming her husband from Aaron's grip, Sue Ellen clung to the body of the man who had claimed her for the sake of the same truce he'd given to Aaron's keeping. "I didn't marry for love but I learned to love you," she whispered. Weeping, she cried out, "Don't leave me!"

"He's gone," pronounced Preacher Green. He closed Judd's open lids, bowed his head, and said with reverence, "Dear Lord, we're a humble people asking You to hear our prayers—"

Hands joined, thirty others swayed along the wave of his chant: "Go in peace, and in peace we be. . . . Go in peace and . . ."

Peace? This was peace, staring in disbelief at his dead father while his mother rocked back and forth, weeping her gratitude for the promise her son hadn't exactly made?

"Aaron, our Aaron, thanks for letting him die easy and leaving no bad blood between you. Bless you for this."

"But, Mama, I—"

The sound of a cocked rifle cut short his entreaty. Aaron turned in the direction of the sound.

A long black iron pointed straight at him, and Uncle Nate demanded, "Goin' back on your word before your papa's had the first shovel of dirt heaped on his grave?"

"Put down the gun." Forcing himself away from the bed, Aaron faced his accuser with a flinty gaze that could have been Papa's own. "Uncle Nate? *Do it.*"

A spit of tobacco to the floor was followed by Uncle Nate's hitch of the shotgun, as he brought a watery eye to the scope.

Were it not for the tear that escaped, Aaron would have called him outside to settle this man-to-man. Instead, he did what he'd learned to do all too well: lock his demons inside a private place that was too damn crowded as it was.

"You're very upset," he said reasonably. "So am I. This obviously isn't a good time to deal with the situation. Let's give it a rest until Papa's buried, then we'll discuss—"

"Nothing to discuss now or later."

Would he shoot his own nephew? Aaron didn't think so. It was just Uncle Nate's way of getting his point across. As for the rest, they backed Nate up with accusations hurled faster than Aaron could deflect them.

"What's wrong, you think those McDonald gals ain't good enough for you?"

"I didn't say that! What I'm saying is—"

"Lots to choose from, gotta be one to strike your fancy."

"*He's* too fancy, that's what he means."

"Maybe Aaron's afraid he'll get his hands dirty touching plain folks such as us. What're you scared of catchin' from one of those McDonald women you swore to marry?"

"Enough, dammit! Put a lid on it and listen to me!" Aaron's shout was rewarded with silence, a silence so absolute, his ears buzzed with it. *Calm, stay calm*, he ordered himself.

"As I was saying, we're all very upset. But we can't let the heat of the moment cloud our judgment. What I see here is . . . a challenge. That's it, a challenge. There comes a time to let grievances go that should've long been forgotten. It's up to us to find a solution, to break free from the past and—and—" *And what?* "Declare ourselves as modern men."

Pausing, Aaron took in those he was addressing, the backdrop of handcrafted furnishings, the spare beauty of the log walls. Primitive but solid and proud was the picture before him. The picture told a story, and it was the story of his life. He loved it. He hated it. Much the same as the bond of admiration and resentment between him and his father.

Putting aside his resentment, Aaron borrowed the stance of authority he knew Papa would use: arms crossed while he waited out the silence.

But assuming his father's posture seemed to set Uncle Elias off. A gnarled finger was suddenly wagging at his face.

"Modern," Elias said with distaste. "You've come a long way, haven't you? So modern that breaking faith with beliefs we take pride in means nothing to you. But there you stand, looking for all the world like Judd. You ain't him, couldn't be in a million years. He's given you the greatest honor he could give, and all that fancy talk can't change the fact that you aim to go back on a sacred trust. You were right—you *don't* deserve it." Shaking his head, he snorted, "Aaron Breedlove, you make me proud that I'm not a modern man."

Uncle Elias, his glare accusing, looked away. And then he turned his back. One by one, Aaron's closest relations gave him their backs, until only his mother remained.

Her face ashen, she begged him, "Aaron, please. *Please?*" She didn't have to say more. He was being shunned, declared worse than dead. It was the mark of Cain. And while he could stroll away without a backward glance, it would be his mother who suffered the sins of her son. Mama had lost her husband this day; she deserved better from him now.

Aaron spoke softly. "I swore to Papa, anything for you." Then his voice rang out over her sobs. "Done! I'll keep the truce, just as our ancestors did. On their graves and that of my father—what was will still be."

He waited, fearful his vow would be refused, but even more afraid that they'd accept his offer.

Uncle Elias turned to face Aaron and his mother. He was the eldest kinsman now that Judson was gone; the rest took their cues from him. All save one.

Jonas spit on the floor, then stalked out, slamming the screen door behind him.

His father should have chosen Jonas, not him. But the choice was made, and far into the night Aaron endured an endless stream of congratulations, condolences, slaps on his back, teary embraces, hesitant and heartfelt welcomes home.

From the corner of his eye he watched his mother tend the husband she'd lost, never stopping except to whisper something that was surely as loving as her touch.

Or perhaps she spoke an assurance that their son had made them proud. Aaron knew better. There was no manly pride in wanting to escape to the far hills.

Even as he touched the silver pieces on his father's eyes, Aaron's thoughts were a mad scramble. He couldn't help but wonder if Papa had felt much the same when *he'd* been named the chosen son.

Surely, no man in his right mind would turn cartwheels for the honor of marrying a woman he didn't want.

TWO

Weddings and wakes, Aaron thought bitterly. It always had been the way of things around here, why should he expect time to make a difference?

He was the chosen son doing time for his transgressions. One would think that getting through last week's funeral and beating himself up with regret for all the hateful words and fights he couldn't take back would be punishment enough. But no, he had to endure the growing certainty that Addy was spoken for, likely had a child or two of her own at the ripe old age of eighteen. She hadn't sought him out to relay her condolences, much less try to rekindle the flame that, despite his best efforts, wouldn't be snuffed.

He hadn't been able to bring himself to ask the questions that assaulted him—"How is Addy? Is she married? Is she happy?" Once answered, they would surely confirm what he didn't want to know. Of course she would be married. And while her lush, beaming smile might fool friends and foes into assuming she was happy, he knew better. Addy could never be happy settling for less than her renegade spirit demanded.

The strain of a fiddle whispered on a pine-scented wind, notes dancing on shadows. It was distant, yet it seemed louder to Aaron than a car alarm set off in the dead of night.

The jug of moonshine set out for the toast was starting to look tempting. Even more tempting was the urge to hurl the damn thing into the ceremonial fire.

"I see the first light," came an expectant whisper. "And there's the second. And the third! Won't be long now—they're well on the trail."

The sound of the fiddle grew louder. The winding stream of flickering candles grew in number. The murmurs of those around him rose in excitement.

Aaron eyed the bottle while his mind worked fast. *Go with the flow until you can haul it back to New York. With a wife. No, not a wife until you consummate the marriage. What you need is a partner in crime. . . .*

Suddenly, silence. And then, the rapid seesaw of the fiddle as its master came into the hallowed clearing.

From the fire's other side he bowed to Aaron, who did what he was sure every chosen son would do—stood to return the bow. And then he heard his mother's sharp whisper.

"Now you sit, and don't get back up till you're ready to choose. Listen sharp, and I'll give you the proper words."

The fiddler swept up from his bow. With a flourish

of his hand, he indicated the sea of candles waving on the cusp of darkness, their peekaboo owners secreted by the forest.

"To the Breedloves, we McDonalds greet you in peace and bring our best offering to keep it."

Mama's whisper caused him to shift uncomfortably. The words he was to speak contained an eloquence that commanded respect. Never mind that he didn't want to be here; here he was. A sense of pride demanded that he do this right.

"The blood on our hands we wash free by mingling ours with that we first took," he repeated with great solemnity.

"Took it you did," the McDonald spokesman concurred. "And we took it back. But there came a time when blood was better shared than shed. . . ."

Despite himself, Aaron was caught up by the gripping drama retold, the heritage of this ritual that had emerged from honor and pride. And death. It was a Breedlove who had taken the life of a McDonald over a mountain they both claimed as theirs. Blood and more blood was let before a bargain was struck between the opposing heads of family: McDonald had several unmarried daughters, and Breedlove had a son who agreed to marry one. Romeo and Juliet they weren't, but the Capulets and Montagues of Half-moon Hollow held their make-do peace. Unfortunately, they also held grudges that wouldn't die.

"Aaron Breedlove, what an honor you bear, chosen as heir to the soil where a river of blood runs deep. A thirsty mountain it is, and bound by duty you are to appease it.

Uphold the truce with the woman you take to wife, and the mountain to the both of you goes. Keep them well, the woman and land that binds you. It's time, chosen son of Half-moon Hollow, to accept this great honor. You *do* accept?"

No! Papa, I'm sorry, so sorry but—

"I . . ." Deep breath, eyes closed. "I do."

"Then take to wife a McDonald by name as your father and the fathers before him did. And the land will belong to neither name till the end of time claims it for heaven."

The tip of the bow pressed to the fiddle's strings an endless chord that was melancholy and sweet. The first McDonald daughter carrying a wavering candle emerged from the dark path and into the fire's light.

She tossed the candle into the fire, and her shy eyes chanced a glance at Aaron's, then lowered in flirtation.

"I'm Esther, and I bring with me the skill of my hands. A good wife I'd be, but if the honor goes to another, then take this sampler I stitched as a wedding present to you and the kin of mine you choose."

One after another the potential wives came forward for consideration. A graceful sway of candles kept time to a feminine parade dressed in their finest, as they moved to the fiddle's seductive refrain. Sleek and fast was his chosen path, but nothing in Aaron's cosmopolitan existence could compete with this array of women moving to a sinuous beat. Even those he readily recognized seemed very different tonight as they blushed prettily, spoke sweetly, and curtsied before the next in line laid down her best offering at his feet.

As the line dwindled, the treasures at his feet grew: dishes from which a tempting aroma tantalized his nostrils, poultices or herbs for a healing tea, tanned hides and dried meat symbolizing the family's wealth of stock grazing the hills. All of the gifts represented some skill or dowry.

The poetry of the ritual, elegant in its simplicity, made a mockery of his earlier cynicism. He was humbled, flattered, and even regretful his other life couldn't possibly accommodate a single one of the women he was offered. Any other man here would surely be in a quandary to select from such a tempting array as this.

While he continued to play the gracious host, his dark depression deepened. No use lying to himself; he'd hoped against hope that by some miracle Addy might be one of the potential brides. It was a crazy wish, of course. He was surely better off without her, considering that the memory of her alone had created such havoc in his life.

From the corner of his eye Aaron thought he glimpsed a familiar dress worn by the last female in the line. But he couldn't give her his full attention without insulting those before her.

Still, he saw enough to put his heart on hold.

Aaron stole another glance. *It had to be Addy*. Who else had hair the color of a raven's wing, a face of innocence promising wickedness, and a royal bearing that begged a man to take her down on a hay-strewn floor, to press kisses to a pair of ill-fitting shoes before losing his very soul inside her.

Despite his best efforts, Aaron's gaze continued to dart to where she stood. Each time he lingered a bit longer, until he was staring while the next-to-last candidate threw the candle down, her gift along with it, and stalked away.

And there she was. Addy, all grown up and taking his breath away without a word between them. Unlike the others, she didn't lower her gaze. And unlike the others, she had no gift of skill in her hands.

Wearing the white cotton sundress that clung tighter than ever, she offered nothing but the slow lift of a button that hung between her breasts. As she stroked it between her fingers, he felt as if she were touching his face, his back—everywhere she'd ever touched him.

What he did not feel was the moral taint he'd wrestled with since that illicit, white-hot night in his father's barn.

"Hello, Addy," he said quietly, intimately.

Candle poised to her lips, she blew a kiss into the flame. Extending him the doused candle, she murmured, "I've thought about you a lot, Aaron. And it pleases me something fierce to see you again."

Oblivious to their audience, he returned her seductively sweet smile and stood to grasp her candle. Their hands touched only briefly, but it was a touch as potent as the memories locked between their searching gazes.

Maybe it was the ritual's captivating aura. Maybe it was the warmth of reunion between two free spirits who might have been friends and lovers had age and circumstance not stood between them. Whatever it was, it was a magic moment.

Until his mother whispered a sharp warning that he wasn't behaving correctly. "And besides, if you want to make up with your brother, you'll leave this girl be. Jonas is hurtin' as it is—don't go rubbing salt in his wounds."

He saw a swift plea in Addy's gaze. *Take me away from here, to that world where you go . . . I won't be any trouble, I promise.* The words still haunted him, and here she was saying them all over again with her eyes.

As he did battle with his conscience for what he hadn't done then and what he was compelled to do now, unease rippled through the crowd while his mother pulled at his arm.

Removing Mama's grip, he announced, "As the chosen son, I say the rules just changed." A collective gasp warned him that he'd better proceed with caution.

"Hear me out, that's all I'm asking." Unwilling to give up the candle that Addy had touched, he pointed it to the chair. "What I see here is a chair that's as special today as it was when my great-grandfather carved it as a wedding present for the wife he chose. But I'm *tired* of sitting. And unless someone can tell me *why* it's so important that I do, then this is one tradition I hereby declare changed!"

Scanning the crowd, he saw a pensive, stunned reaction. His demand had been minor, yet anything but. He had called for change, and in Half-moon Hollow that posed no little threat. Few Appalachian hamlets remained—the unique way of life they revered was dying. How well he understood the need to protect what was theirs, even after spending more than a decade resenting the origins to which he owed his success.

Aaron Breedlove, the icon of primitive art.

Something primitive stirred inside him. Addy's eyes

sparkled with an adulation so fierce, he felt as if she'd vaulted him to the sky. No human could be exalted so high without suffering a great fall, but he wanted to revel in her misplaced awe while he still could.

He turned to her, saying, "Your competition's had their turn, now it's yours. Convince me why I should choose you and not one of them." A discreet snap of his teeth. "*Convince me.*"

A spark of determination kindled her gaze to a promised fire as she slowly lifted a hand to untie the bow at the back of her neck. The strap fell forward, and he fought the instinct to push it back up before she fell out. *He wanted to see her breasts.* But he didn't want anyone else to see. To his relief, the fit was so tight that the bodice stayed put.

She began to move. *Dear heaven and hell the woman could move.* Hypnotized by her sustained sway, Aaron thought he heard the beat of tapping feet. But the sound was a distant echo, far away from this private show meant only for him. This ballad was so achingly personal that it could only be for him.

As Addy sang, she moved closer and closer until the tips of her battered shoes touched the fine leather of his. She ended the song on a note so soft, only he could hear it. She was so near that only he saw her palm stroke down his chest as she whispered, "You want me. Try to deny it and, in front of God and your mama, I'll prove it right here."

Aaron sat down so fast, he nearly toppled back the chair.

"If I didn't convince you, then choose the one who

did," she continued in a hushed, suggestive tone. "But if you do choose me, well, since you're to make your choice known with a kiss, make sure it's plenty good. I have waited four years for it."

With that Addy yanked free the embroidery thread from her throat and tossed the button into his lap.

Button, button, who's got the button? Button, hell, it felt like a hot potato wedged in his crotch. Discreetly as he could, Aaron transferred it to his shirt pocket. He looked up in time to see Addy smirk slightly before she strolled away with that sexy, aloof walk of hers that made him want to kiss her senseless.

He wanted to applaud. He wanted to throw his head back and howl with laughter. *He wanted to tackle Addy and teach her that lesson she still needed to learn.*

"Ahem." The McDonald spokesman cleared his throat, as did several others. Everyone else appeared speechless. It was Aaron's guess that another century-old tradition had just been broken, and Addy had done it in a New York minute. No, he didn't think her suggestion of a striptease and an all-but-public seduction would be condoned by the elders present, much less the ancestors who had held court in this scared clearing.

"Aaron Breedlove, chosen son of Judson, take your pick of these good women whose honor it'd be to spend their days as your wife. McDonalds and Breedloves alike bless you both for the peace it brings to us all." Then, leaning close, he said confidentially, "You want to think a spell? I'll be glad to play my fiddle while you chew on it."

"Thanks all the same, but no chewing needed," Aaron said as he stood up.

As soon as he did, his mother hissed at his back, "There's a pecking order here, if you didn't take notice. Even if you're not feeling generous toward Jonas—"

"Where's your own generosity, Mama?" Meeting her reproachful gaze, he whispered, "Seems I recall Papa saying you were the last in line yourself." After gentling his rebuke with a kiss to her cheek, Aaron went straight for the first in line.

"Thank you, Esther. Your sampler was beautiful, and so are you. Some man's going to be mighty lucky to have you for a wife." Pausing here, lingering there, down the line he went, extending his thanks to each one.

But it was to Addy he paid his briefest regards.

"Thanks for the reminder and the song. Damn good show." He withdrew the button from his pocket and pressed it into her palm, then folded her fingers. "Catch you later . . . little girl."

Addy's slight smile wavered. He left her with a wink.

Returning to the esteemed chair, he swiveled it to face the great mountain of towering evergreens reaching for the moon. His gaze drawn there, he could have sworn the man-in-the-moon winked.

Looking around, Aaron faced the witnesses who expectantly strained forward, as he announced, "I have chosen the woman I would ask to be my wife."

Aaron turned his gaze to Addy.

"Addy McDonald. My arms are open. Come into them and share a mountain and more with the chosen son who has chosen you for his bride. And with our vows, may both sides of Half-moon Hollow live in peace for the duration of our lives."

She took one step in his direction, then two, and Aaron knew the battle of his life had just ensued.

She fell into his arms and tilted her mouth to his.

He told himself that a kiss was far from a consummation. He told himself that a kiss was just a kiss even if the one he wanted from Addy was hotter than sex, stronger than the white lightning awaiting their ritual sip of the bottle.

The want had never left him. And what was want, but a wish that refused to die?

As he lowered his mouth to hers, Aaron saw a star fall.

THREE

Addy's heart was so full, it was near to overflowing. Her prince had come! And she was Cinderella taken into his arms.

His breath held the power of fairy dust blown against her lips. His fingers thrusting into her hair were magic wands casting a spell of shimmering sensation. And his whisper of "Kiss me" mingled with the sound of trumpets on the wind.

At the first touch of his mouth Addy's heart leaped so hard and high, she was sure it shot clear to heaven. Her head was light, her body heavy and sinking against his. A shower of rainbow lights danced behind her eyelids. *Was this real?*

Aaron's muffled groan seemed real enough. As for his mouth, it was firm yet soft. Then he dipped her back, and his teasing lips opened wide over hers, demanding ownership of her mouth and leaving no doubt this kiss was definitely real!

He kissed like a worldly man who knew what he wanted, and what he wanted was ferocious and hot—so hot that he could have melted ore with a single sweep of his tongue. Her flesh felt on fire, and she vaguely wondered if a woman could die from a kiss.

If so, how blessed it was to burn at his stake, to meet her end in Aaron's tender, consuming embrace.

"Addy . . . *Addy?*"

Warm breath tickling her ear, she murmured, "Huh?"

"Are you all right? Talk to me, Addy!"

She felt a light pat to her cheek urging her to swim up from a pool of liquid sensation. Her vision smoky, she murmured, "Mmmm, Aaron, that was one fine kiss."

Nuzzling against his neck, she wondered when he'd picked her up. No matter, she was his bride-to-be, and come the next half-moon he'd be carrying her over the threshold. But she couldn't wait that long for another taste of his mouth. "Kiss me again?" she asked with a sigh.

"I think we'd better hold off until you recover from the first one." He smiled a slow, cocky smile, if ever she'd seen one.

"You're certainly looking pleased with yourself," she said tartly, miffed that he hadn't readily obliged her.

"Believe me, I am." His eyes, dancing a jig of victory, had nothing on his preening tone. "It's not every day a man can make a woman faint from something as simple as a kiss."

"Faint? *Faint!*" Addy decided he was baiting her in

one of their old games of will, an affectionate tit for tat.

"I did *not* faint," she haughtily informed him.

"Did," he countered with a laugh.

"Did not, you jackass."

"Watch your tongue, Addy. I like it a whole lot better dripping honey than vinegar." He stopped laughing, but his smirk stayed put, making her wonder if Aaron did have a streak of arrogance in him. If so, she aimed to get rid of it and proceeded to do just that with a sly slip of her tongue between his lips. He muttered a soft curse, and her gaze softened under the heat of his.

Addy touched his cheek. Aaron jerked away as if her fingertips were lit matches.

"Think you can stand up now?" he asked gruffly.

Something wasn't right, she realized with a sudden alarm. For some reason he was anxious to put some distance between them and reluctant to do it at the same time. At her slight nod he lowered her down his length, slow as syrup trickling from a maple tree in midwinter.

She took a step back, and upon hearing his sigh of relief, she pretended dizziness and fell forward. Her breasts bore down on his chest, and she could feel the heavy thud of his racing heartbeat. Quickly, he gripped her waist and steadied her, pulling away as he did.

"Thank you, Aaron," she said with a throaty whisper. "Maybe we shouldn't touch much more than we kiss."

As for Aaron, he didn't look anywhere close to fainting. More like a keg of dynamite set to go off with a single, intimate touch to his short fuse.

"Ready to get on with this?" he asked gruffly.

She searched his eyes, praying she'd see the eagerness that his voice lacked. What she saw was a battlefield of yearning and regret. As his palm came to rest on her shoulder, his touch told her more than his gaze: He wanted her, he cared for her, but he did *not* want to marry her.

Addy's heart plummeted. She felt like Cinderella, winning the prince because her foot had luckily fit. She wanted him to beg her to be his bride, even if her shoe size didn't match that of the glass slipper.

Forcing her head high and freezing her smile in place, she refused to let her hurt show.

"Bring on the jug!" Aaron's voice rang out with a solemnity befitting the occasion. Accepting the jug, he bowed to her. "A toast to Addy McDonald, my soon-to-be bride. If you'll do me that honor, then commit yourself with a sip."

He extended her the bottle. Addy hesitated, wanting this more than anything but not like this.

"Take it," he whispered urgently. "Addy, I'm counting on you. Please, don't let me down."

She didn't have much choice, not really, because if she refused his offer, he'd have to pick another bride. As she took the first sip, the white lightning whistled through her head and brought tears to her eyes.

She endured Aaron's touch on her hand as he took too long to accept the jug that signified their troth. He mouthed "Thank you," and she acknowledged him with a curt nod.

The tip of the jug to his mouth was brisk, as was his quick swallow. A shudder ran through him, and Addy feared it was less from the corn liquor's bite than it was from the binding promise he'd just made to marry her.

A mass whoop of jubilation went up as Sue Ellen took the next swig. From mouth to mouth the jug was passed until it was empty and several others were brought forth.

With the celebration in full swing, Aaron reached for her hand. She returned his squeeze, closing her eyes.

Without a word between them she believed they understood what the other was feeling. Aaron had no choice but to marry her, a woman he wanted against his will.

As for her, she was claiming a dream that fell far short of what she'd dreamed it would be.

FOUR

"Aren't you excited, Addy? Why, this time tomorrow night you'll be wedded and dancing with your groom."

Paying more attention than need be to folding the friendship quilt presented her by the clan of McDonald women that day, Addy said evasively, "All these names threaded in—can't help but wonder if a couple might feel crowded in bed."

"Reckon you'll find out soon enough," Loretta teased. "Could be you'll be glad for that bit of company from home once you're in New York."

"New York," Addy repeated, feeling both anxiety and awe. "Aaron says they don't even use outhouses there, no lake around, either, to take a skinny-dip bath. And there's all sorts of places to go and things to do, Aaron says, and—"

"Aaron sez this, Aaron sez that," Loretta mimicked, spitting out his name. "When are you gonna start talking for yourself again? Far as I can see, you two ain't spoken three words in private since he asked you to be his wife. Day after day I see you smile at the gatherings, then tuck your presents away under our bed with a sniff. And don't think for a minute I don't hear you bawlin' in your pillow once you think I'm asleep. What are you cryin' for, Addy?" she demanded.

"Oh, Loretta, it's awful," she blurted out, tears springing to her eyes. "Aaron doesn't want to marry me, and I keep telling myself that I can make him love me back the way I've always loved him. But this other voice in my head says that's a lie, that I'm spitting in the wind because nobody can make someone feel something that's not there."

"But, Addy, he does feel something, and that something's mighty strong. The way that man looks at you gives me the shivers, and if I was you, I'd be plumb scared to crawl under the covers with him tomorrow night."

"He wants me—you're right about that." Brushing away the tears she had no use for, Addy clenched her jaw. "But, Loretta, that's settling, and I want more. For as long as I can remember, Aaron's been everything I ever wanted to be."

"Besides being rich, fancy-mannered, and the sort that keeps to himself, what's he got that you don't?"

"A lot. He's patient and he's generous and wise and—"

"And how do you know that for sure? Think about it, Addy, how well do you *really* know Aaron?"

"What kind of question is *that*?" Addy demanded. "Being the only person—besides him—that I ever told my secrets to, you should know well how I know. Ever since Aaron saved me from that rattler just before he struck out on his own, I knew he was the only one for me."

"Then you knew a lot more than most six-year-olds do."

"Well, could be that I wasn't exactly sure then," she admitted, "but every year that Aaron came back, I was more and more sure. He brought me the world with the books he read to me, then gave me to keep, the fancy clothes he said that he picked out just for me, because pretty as I was, I deserved better than a flour-sack dress. And when everybody else laughed at the songs I made up, it was Aaron who clapped when I sang just for him. Aaron told me I had a gift and that he was proud of me. And—and, don't forget the china doll he gave me for my twelfth birthday—"

"Along with a promise that he'd carve a dollhouse, a house as grand as the one you belonged in," Loretta supplied with a gentle smile. "But he never did. Why not?"

Addy hesitated to explain. There had been a condition that Aaron had attached. The dollhouse would be his present for her sixteenth birthday—just so she would be willing to swear on a stack of Bibles that she was sweet sixteen and never been kissed. Given their horrible parting, it was no small surprise that the dollhouse had never come to pass.

"Could be that he decided to wait till we had a house of our own to share," she hedged.

"That's hogwash, Addy, and you know it. The point is, Aaron might be wise and patient as a sort of big brother or a favorite uncle, but he could be a whole lot different as a husband. Much as I hate to say it, I don't think that you really know the man at all."

A creeping suspicion that just maybe Loretta was right caused Addy to frown. "Are you telling me that you think I'm about to marry a stranger?" she asked.

"What I'm saying is that the man you love is likely a far cry from the man you're about to be stuck with. Mark my words, the both of you have a lot to learn about each other before either of you can fall in love for real."

Addy was terribly afraid that her sister was right. After all, the Aaron she'd always looked up to and loved so dearly never would have made her dream come true only to smash it apart.

He had deserted her when she needed him—it was as simple as that. The despair she'd been battling coursed into a swift anger at the man who had let her down.

"Seems that I haven't been able to see the forest for the trees," she finally said. Her hands balling into fists, Addy began to pace the small room. "So tell me, Loretta, what's a woman to do once she's wedded to a man instead of a memory?"

"Be strong. And strong you are, Addy. One of the strongest people I know."

Addy knew that she'd have to be strong to put the past in its proper place and forge bravely ahead into the future.

"It's not going to be easy," she muttered. "But anything worth having is worth fighting for. Fact is, lots of folks get married to strangers—they just don't realize it till the honeymoon's over."

Encouraged by Loretta's hearty nod, she rushed on. "Aaron wants me for a fact. And even if he's not in love with me—yet—I know he likes me. Two out of three ain't bad."

"That's the spirit, Addy!"

Feeling better already, she said with a smile, "Now that that's settled, we'd best get some sleep. After all, I won't be getting much tomorrow night."

Long after Loretta was dozing, Addy stared at the wedding dress hanging near the window. A soft breeze fluttered the lace on the gown that other brides had worn before her. Had they lain awake full of hopes and dreams carried on a wing and a prayer? Or had they gathered their strength to face an uncertain future with a man they hardly knew?

When sleep finally came, there were no tears on Addy's pillow.

The wedding suit his ancestors had worn felt disturbingly at home on Aaron's frame. Even the high starched neck of the formal shirt had an eerie feel of belonging.

Sitting beneath a familiar old tree, he released a deep sigh. An hour from now it would all be over—except for the biggest hurdle of all: the wedding bed.

A quick sweat beaded his brow. Before he could wipe it off, a square of white cotton was dangled in front of his face.

"What's wrong, brother? Seems you're sweatin' already."

Jonas squatted beside him, beneath the tree they'd climbed as boys. Less than a year between them, they'd grown up so close only to end up a world apart.

"Mama send you to find me, or does that white kerchief mean you came to call a truce on your own?"

Dropping the handkerchief in Aaron's lap, he said tightly, "You had your pick, why'd you have to take Addy?"

"Because it was the right thing to do, Jonas."

"But you don't even want her!"

"You're wrong about that." Picking up a twig, he twirled it, and for a moment all he could see was a sundress floating around bare legs in a barn. "I do want her."

"So do I. She'd be mine if you'd shown up a day later."

"If you'd been the chosen son, you could have married her. But, Jonas, that doesn't mean she would have been yours. She'd have to love you for that ever to happen."

"And I suppose Addy McDonald loves you," Jonas shot back.

"She *thinks* she's in love with me. There's a big difference between an adolescent crush and the real thing." Aaron snapped the twig and threw it on the ground. "You have to know someone to love them, and Addy has a lot to learn about me. My guess is, it's only a matter of time before she wants to get free of me and packs her bags."

Even as he said what he knew was true, he couldn't help but dread it already. When Jonas asked hopefully,

"Think there's a chance she might head back in this direction?" Aaron gave some thought to his answer.

"Could be. She's got her head filled with a pipe dream, and the reality of it is, she's got a tough row to hoe. Then again, Addy's a survivor at heart." So was he, but he had a bad feeling that his heart might not survive Addy.

That much he kept to himself. Wanting to make the best peace he could with his brother, Aaron waved the handkerchief.

"It should have been you, not me, chosen to keep the truce. Everyone else knows it too, Jonas. Since they'd rather have the head clansman close by, think you could stand in for me and hold down the fort while I'm gone?"

Slapping his palm against Aaron's, Jonas said in a choked voice, "Seems that Papa did choose the better man. Mind if I stand up with you in front of Preacher Green?"

"The only one who'd like that better than me would be Mama." Getting up, the brothers reunited with a bear hug. As they did, Aaron felt dewdrops sprinkle through the trees. "Ah, crap, don't tell me we've got rain on the way."

"Rain? What rain? No birds flyin' low, no earthworms snaking over the ground. And no one's said they spotted a black snake in a tree. Got at least three days of sun accordin' to the signs."

"Uh . . . right."

As they walked through the forest, half-moon on the rise, Aaron was compelled to ask, "Do you love Addy, Jonas?"

"I could learn to. Even from a distance I've fancied her for a long time—me and every other man around. You?"

"What's love got to do with it?" He thought briefly of Claudia, but he knew love didn't have any part in their relationship. It was the best thing about their affair—neither of them stood to get hurt.

Picking up his pace, Aaron felt an unsettling eagerness set in as the wedding site loomed near. He abruptly stopped at trail's end.

Firelight rippled over her, her waist-length hair cascading like a sable cloak over the pale shadow of vintage silk. Her hair. How many times had he imagined brushing it, running his fingers through it, burying his face in it. . . .

"Just look at her there," Jonas whispered in awe. "How could any man not love a woman like that? Lord, but she looks like an angel."

Aaron sucked in a deep breath and said, "If Addy's an angel, then I'm a saint. She's hell on wheels, and if I'm not careful, she's sure to burn rubber down my back." His forward step was cut short by a hand on his shoulder.

"You never answered me, Brother. Could you love her?"

Unable to take his eyes off Addy, Aaron confessed, "I've loved her since she was a little girl who looked up at me like I hung the moon. But she's outgrown that kind of love. I can only pray that I never love her as a woman."

"Why not? She's going to be your wife."

His wife. A mate for life who shared hopes and dreams, tears and laughter, affection and fights. How he wanted that, *needed* it. But it couldn't be with Addy. He couldn't even let himself think it.

"Only a very foolish man would risk such a thing. You see, Jonas, it's only a matter of time before Addy outgrows her need for me." Breaking from Jonas's grip, Aaron moved as if by compulsion and whispered, "Dear Lord, don't let me love her that way, not ever. Have enough mercy to spare me that."

FIVE

Beneath the half-moon, fiddles and banjos swung from a waltz to a stompin' good ditty, with the rhythmic blow of several moonshine bottles joining in. With each new song Aaron's jaw grew tighter as he watched Addy passed from one dancing partner to another. A dip and her hair swept the ground.

Damn her, did she have to laugh with such abandon, smile at every man but him? Working the ring on his hand, he still felt the sizzling hold of her touch when she'd slid it down his finger. Not that she'd looked at him when she did it—hell, she hadn't looked at him all night!

And as for that wedding kiss . . .

Aaron hissed out a curse just thinking about that chaste little peck, and the way Addy had stepped away from him when he impulsively reached for her. He'd salved his ego by telling himself she was afraid she might faint—which was surely the same reason she'd avoided so much as a single, questioning touch. *Right.*

"Swig?" Eyeing the offered jug, Aaron wondered if he dared. One good swallow and maybe he'd pass out before he did something stupid. *Real* stupid, like taking her to bed and ridding himself of the ache that no other woman had been able to appease, unless he shut his eyes and pretended it was Addy on a pile of hay.

"Thanks all the same, but I've hit my limit." His gaze narrowed on her, and he didn't turn toward the elbow at his ribs.

"If I was you, I'd be savin' myself up too. Hey, boys?"

"Got that right!"

"Heaven take me to the Pearly Gates. One taste of Addy's lips, and I'd die a happy man."

"Excuse me?" Aaron jabbed a finger in the last speaker's chest and in a cold whisper said, "I'm sure you must be talking about some other gal, not my wife."

"Tha-that's right. Uh, I was uh, speakin' of Loretta."

"That's my wife's sister, and my brother's been dancing with her most of the night. Maybe I should call Jonas over and see what he—"

"Hang on there, Aaron." Uncle Ephram wedged himself in the middle. "Caleb here was just foolin', weren't you, boy?"

"Just fooling, that's right. Sorry, Aaron, I don't want a fight. It was the whiskey talking, not me." He put out his hand. A few tense seconds passed before Aaron gripped it.

"Enjoy the party. If you'll excuse me, it's time I saw to my wife." He nodded to the circle of kinsmen that had formed around them. "Gentlemen."

As he strode away, Aaron muttered, "Wife? *Wife!*" He'd actually called Addy his wife! Not once, not twice, but three times he'd called her his wife! Lord, he had to be insane. If he didn't get a grip on himself, both he and Addy were going to be in some very serious trouble.

Aaron clamped his hand down on her current partner's shoulder. As he whirled around, cousin Luke's scowl vanished, and a grin split his face.

"Well, if it isn't the groom himself cutting in to dance with his bride." A slap to Aaron's back, and Luke bowed out with a chuckle. "She's all yours, you lucky dog."

All his. From the defiant lift of her delicate chin to the rapid rise and fall of her breasts to the impatient tap of her toes, the hellion bride was his.

"Dance, Addy?" Aaron asked shortly.

Raising her eyes to his, she sniffed. "My feet are a bit tired. Think I'll sit this one out."

She stepped away, and Aaron caught her arm. He pulled her against him and accused, "You've danced with everyone but me."

"Guess that's why I'm fresh out of energy."

Scowling, Aaron bent down to take the wedding kiss he'd been cheated out of. Addy gave him her cheek.

"That does it!" And with that, he hoisted her roughly over his shoulder.

"What do you think you're doing? Put me down, you hear?" Caressing her behind, he cut an aggressive path through the crowd.

"Damn you, Aaron Breedlove, I *said*, put me down! And—and, stop that!"

Another caress and he informed her, "I'll stop it when I damn well please, and as for putting you down, I wouldn't *dream* of making you walk when you're fresh out of energy."

Addy's protests were drowned out by the good-natured heckles that followed them to the edge of the forest. From there, Aaron made tracks. He didn't stop until he got to his parents' house, vacated for the night.

He kicked the bedroom door open, went directly to the bed, and dropped Addy onto the feather mattress.

He quickly lit an oil lamp. Arms folded and legs braced wide, he loomed over her from the side of the bed.

"Okay. Let's have it, Addy."

"Have what?" she said tartly.

"Have it out, that's what." When she warily eyed his crotch, he stifled a chuckle, a groan, and gave her a wicked half-smile.

Addy primly pushed down the hem from her knees to her feet. Her gaze darted to the door. Unable to resist feeding her anxiety, Aaron strolled over and hooked the latch.

Leaning back, he suggestively lifted a brow. "Not that we should have any unexpected company, but, just in case. Who knows, you might take to screaming or . . . fighting or . . . even fainting while we have it out." And then, with a leer and a wink. "Ready? I am, even if you're not."

Even from where he stood, he could see her heart-in-throat swallow. He pulled off his boots, then with slow, measured paces stalked her with a feral gleam in his eyes. By the time his shins hit bed's end, Addy had scooted away and was shaking her head.

"Not—not ready!" she squeaked.

"Not ready?" he repeated softly, reaching for her feet. While slipping off her shoes, he said in a warning whisper, "But, Addy, your *groom* is ready, and do you know what that means?" Gripping her ankles, he drew her down to the foot of the bed and roared, "That means we're having it out!"

"Beast!" she yelped, landing shimmy kicks to his knees. When he blocked them with a spread of her legs, she wailed at the ceiling, "Beast!"

"Damn right," he growled, lowering his face toward hers. "Where the hell do you get off treating me like that in public? Lady, I'm pissed, so you'd better listen up: Don't you *ever* thumb your nose at me like that again. And on top of that, if you're too tired to dance with me, then consider yourself too tired to dance with anyone else. You got that?"

Addy's look of surprise gave way to an overwhelming sense of relief. Before he could crack a smile, she gave him a go-to-hell look. Her cheeks were bright splotches of red. Wiggling away from him and getting to her feet, she pushed him to the floor and glowered down at him.

"I'll tell you what I've got. *Pride*. Not that you left me much, Mr. High and Mighty Chosen Son who chose himself a bride he didn't want and stayed away from *me* like the pox for the last two weeks! You spoke your piece, now I'll give you mine, Aaron Breedlove. My face hurts from smiling, and my neck hurts from holding my head up when all I wanted to do was hide it under a rock. Don't *you* ever shame me like that in public again. *You* got that?"

He was guilty, and he knew it.

"Confession time, Addy." He steeled himself to lay the first bone bare. "I hate apologizing as much as I hate being wrong. But it was wrong of me to be distant with you. You're upset, and rightfully so. I'm sorry."

"In that case . . . so am I." Her eyes searched his. "But that doesn't explain why you ignored me."

Where to start, how much to reveal? Finally, he said, "I had a lot of thinking to do. It's hard for me to think clearly when I'm around you." Hell, when it came to Addy, he couldn't think clearly whether she was there or not. But here she was, fairly glowing at his words and casting a shy yet eager glance at the bed. Oh, this was going to be even worse than he'd feared.

"There's another reason, Addy. When I see you, I want to touch you. And so I stayed away to avoid the temptation."

Her lids drooped seductively. "My, what a fine gentleman you are, Aaron Breedlove, and how lucky I am to have you. How many men would keep their distance to honor the virtue of a woman before taking her to wife? I *was* sweet sixteen, Aaron. And though I've had my share of kisses since then, I saved myself for you. I'm yours for the taking."

Dropping to her knees, she kissed his wedding ring, then pressed his palm to her heart. The fullness of her breast beneath his hand wrenched a deep groan from his throat. He knew he was courting disaster, but the need to touch her was too strong to be denied.

Sliding his palm down, he cupped her and gently, possessively squeezed. He could feel the heat of her flesh beneath the satin, could feel the very thrum of her blood colliding with his in a headlong, feverish rush.

"Dear God, how I want you."

"Then what are you waiting for? It's our wedding night, Aaron. You're my husband, and I'm your wife. Take me," she murmured. She moaned softly and then urgently demanded, *"Take me."*

SIX

There was a desperate hunger in his lingering caress. Even more desperate was the low groan he made as he slowly withdrew his touch.

His lips were so close to her ear, she felt the fine hair prickle at her nape as he whispered, "I'm sorry for hurting you before, even more sorry for the hurt to come." Aaron raked his fingers through her hair, then gathered it up and wrapped it about his neck.

A soft tug and his nose met hers. "My pearl."

"Pearl?" she repeated on a sigh. Then, remembering he was about to hurt her somehow, she asked warily, "Why pearl?"

"Quite simply, a pearl is what you are. A rare pearl that's grown in a hiding place, tight as a closed oyster. I'm the fisherman who's claimed you from his net—and I'm so hungry that I'm afraid I'll try to swallow my find instead of sharing you with others who'll recognize your worth." He pressed a kiss to her temple. "Do you understand?"

"Let me see. I'm a pearl. You're a fisherman who wants to eat me. But there's others out there you want to share me with because they'll think me to be worth something and—" She gasped, horrified. "Surely, you don't aim to sell me off once we leave here?"

"Oh, Addy," he said with a weary laugh. "Pearl be damned, you're a diamond in the rough and cutting me to the quick." He framed her jaw with his palm as he told her, "No one could ever buy you, Addy. You belong to yourself and no one else."

"But that's not true! As your wife, I belong to you."

"Don't I wish." Sadly, he shook his head. "But wishing won't make the impossible happen." She wanted to set his mind at ease and prove without a doubt that she most certainly did belong to him. She wanted to touch his vast, manly chest, to feel his heart beat.

He was so still, not a single breath passed his lips while she took off his tie and undid several buttons. But when she reached the one nudging his belt, he grabbed her wrist.

"*No.*" For one wanting to sound so sure of himself, Aaron didn't sound at all as if he meant it. Addy forgot the button and pressed a fingertip into his navel. His stomach muscles flexed beneath her touch, and he said sharply, "Don't do that."

"Why not?" The hardness of his belly brought a fluttering in her own. Claiming the right to touch him however she liked, she stroked the fine hair that edged his trousers.

"Sweet Jesus," he whispered with reverence.

"Aaron? You okay?"

"Oh baby, never better." His belly tensed under her palm.

"You sound closer to worse than better. Are you ill?" Addy brushed back a shock of fine, pale hair and pressed her cheek to his forehead. "No fever," she pronounced.

"Oh, I've got a fever, and it's about to burn me alive. But . . . no. *No.* I'm having a real struggle here. Help me out, babe. *Please?*"

He was begging her to help him, and when he put it so needfully, she couldn't refuse him. Or herself.

"There now, Aaron, don't you worry about me," she murmured as she slid the leather of his belt through the gold buckle. "I know we had a fight and all, and I'm sure it won't be the last. But this is our honeymoon night, and I'm more than ready to kiss and make up. As for that fever of yours, it'd be my pleasure to tend those flames about to burn you alive."

"Forget the fever," he panted as she slid down his zipper. "Addy, you're killing me by inches."

"Don't die on me now, Aaron. I know you want me and, to tell the truth, I want you too. Bad, I want you so bad—"

"Please, Lord," he breathed, "tell me what to do."

"I figured you did, but if you don't, no need to pray for instruction." Laying open his pants, Addy stared at what looked to be a wild jungle print in green and pink on his briefs. "Um, seems to me it—it shouldn't be much different from the way animals breed," she said unsteadily.

Aaron went from a mass of tight muscle to a total slump.

"You have no idea how . . . how hard this is for me to—to say, but . . ." Arm thrown over his face, he gnashed out, "Addy, we can't, *cannot*, make love."

"Not make love?" she repeated. "Why not, Aaron?" More than confused, she was driven by a need to touch him everywhere. Soft as a summer breeze, she traced his hidden flesh, only for it to grow beneath her fingertips. She gasped in delight, yet Aaron seemed to be in the throes of agony.

"Does it hurt?" she asked gently. "If it does, a kiss is sure to make it better."

"Don't! Don't kiss me there!"

His hips were arching up as he pushed her hand away, while he licked at her lips as if they were the last drop of the finest elderberry wine.

"You're telling me no with your words and shouting yes everywhere else," she got out between his nibbling kisses. "Aaron, whatever is the matter with you?"

"Annulment," he wheezed out. "Sweet heaven, Addy, I want you so much that I'd give up five years of my life for one minute inside you right now. But now isn't forever, and this is one deal we can't seal."

With a curse he bounded to his feet and began to pace.

Something dreadful and chilly shot from her head to her heart as she forced herself to ask, "What deal? The only one I know of is our marriage and the truce between our families. I don't know what annulment means." Swallowing hard, she said, "Don't think I want to."

"Believe me, it's not something I want to explain any more than you want to hear it." He paused at the oil lamp. His eyes were full of conflicting emotions, and heaven knew she was battling to stay calm. He put out the light, as if he couldn't bear to look at her and see the confusion and dread sure to be etched on her face.

The moon shone behind his back as he came toward her. "An annulment isn't quite as bad as breaking a promise," he said slowly. "It's more like, well, the promise wasn't thought out, and the people who made it decide to pretend it never existed. Does that make sense?"

"Sounds like nonsense to me. Sounds like an Indian giver wanting the blessing of the person he stole his gift back from."

"Not exactly. You see, both of them have to agree that they made a mistake." He crouched down and leaned so close that she could see the regret in his gaze. "It would be a terrible mistake for us to consummate this marriage."

"Consummate." She tried the word out and liked its solid feel. But she didn't care at all for the look-but-don't-touch emphasis Aaron had put on it. "You mean . . . sex."

"That's right. But if a partner is denied intimate rights, then there's just cause to erase the marriage without a divorce."

Divorce? Their vows were just spoken, and Aaron was already thinking about divorce? The chill she'd felt was nothing compared to the icy waters he was drowning her in now. She was seized by a frantic instinct to escape the betrayal of this trusted friend she had loved blindly and would surely learn to love all over again if only he would let her know him as a man, a husband. A lover. And here he was, giving her no hope. Not even the crumb of a consoling touch.

"Do you hate me so much, Aaron?" Addy searched his eyes, silently begging him to take back his treachery.

"Hate you?" he said in disbelief. "I could never hate you. *Never*. I care for you. Deeply. I always have."

"And you call this caring? Refusing to share a bed with me, telling me our marriage is over before it even gets started?" When he touched a tear she hadn't realized was there, she knocked away his hand. Her voice shaking with unbridled emotion, she charged, "I'd think you cared more if you slapped me instead."

At the moment she would have preferred a slap to wake her from this living nightmare. Instead he claimed her left hand, slowly rubbing her gold wedding band. He'd have to cut it off before she'd give it up, she thought to herself.

"Maybe not just yet, but there will come a day that you'll want this gone. It won't take long for you to figure out that it's freedom, not me, you really want. An annulment might seem nasty now, but it could be a relief once you've had a chance to get some distance." He cupped her face, and there was such an ache in his touch that she knew he was hurting as badly as she. "This marriage, Addy, it can't possibly work."

He looked as if he wanted to cry the tears she unwillingly shed. He caught one of the tears on her cheek with the tip of his finger.

"How can you be so sure that it won't work?" she demanded, praying for a protective anger that wouldn't come.

"Because I've been where you're about to go. Though you can't see what's coming, I do—all too clearly."

"And just what do you see?"

"A fatal accident that's awful to witness, but no matter how hard I try to look away, I can't. You're a survivor. But if I'm to survive, too, we can't take so much as a joy ride together. If we do, I'll look away from the wheel, and while I'm staring with stars in my eyes at you, reality will hit us head-on. *Boom*. Crash and burn, you know?"

"I *don't* know and—and all I care about is that you're turning me away when all I want is to be a wife to you."

He sighed heavily and plowed a hand through his hair. "Look, Addy, please, try to understand that you're young and naive, everything that I'm not. You're beautiful and you're special and any man's dream—"

"*Your* dream, too, I suppose." Her snort of derision mocked the despair that sliced through her sharp as a knife.

"Of course you are," he hastened to assure her. "But dreams aren't reality. That's why I'm doing my damndest to protect us from chasing a dream that just can't be."

"Keep your damn protection! I don't want it any more than I need it. And as for dreams, they're as real as rainbows. You can see rainbows, and if you reach long and high enough—"

"You'll still never find a pot of gold at the end."

Desperate to make him see the beauty of a dream that *could* be if only he, too, would believe, she asked him in an accusing whisper, "And just when was the last time you tried?"

He met her challenging gaze only briefly before he got to his feet and went to the open window. His fists braced against either side of the frame, Aaron seemed more distant than the faint sound of celebratory laughter drifting into the room.

Aching to touch him, she was too poignantly reminded of another place, another time. Then, as now, she felt desperate, hurt, deserted. Had she been that same girl in the barn, she would have been tempted to hurl a fistful of dried dung at him.

But she wasn't that girl—she was a woman of purpose and passion. Determined to make Aaron realize it, she went to him. But she didn't circle her arms around him. She didn't press her cheek between his tensed shoulders.

"Remember what I told you that night in the barn, about being careful for what you ask?" he softly warned. "The advice still holds. Keep pushing, and you're liable to get more than what you bargained for—in bed and out. Do us both a favor? Back off."

"No." And then she did put her arms around him, sweeping her cheek over the thin, starched fabric of the aged dress shirt. Simply, she asked him, "Who are you?"

His head fell forward, and he shook it. "Depends

on who you ask. You'll get almost as many answers as there are people I know. I don't let anyone get too close."

"But I'm not asking them. I'm asking you."

Hard as it was, she waited out his silence until he said quietly, "I'm not who or what you think I am. You married a dream, not a man."

"Then tell me about the man."

"He's no hero, babe." His short bark of laughter made her wince, and yet there he suddenly was, turning, returning her embrace, and saying, "For this once let me be the hero that I'm not. You can have the bed. I'll take the floor."

"But I don't want the bed, not unless you're stealing the covers," she protested. "Besides, I don't remember pledging my life to a hero, but to a man."

"Addy, you married a stranger."

"So did you," she countered. "If you didn't notice, I'm even harder to run off now than I used to be."

He laughed a little at that. "Now who's scared?"

"You? That'd surely be a first."

Aaron raised a brow.

With that simple, unspoken admission she felt her heart lift. It was more than the small access he'd given her to the man he really was, it was the knowledge that she had some sort of hold over Aaron that frightened him—at least enough for him to say gruffly, "Quit looking at me that way."

"What way?" she drawled, and ran her thumb along his bottom lip.

"Like you've won a battle, that's how." He gripped her wrist. His eyes narrowed, and he bit softly into her palm. "You're trespassing on dangerous ground. Be careful, or you're liable to win the battle only to lose the war."

Again he took a bite, only sharper, so that she let go a startled gasp.

"Consider that a warning," he murmured in a dark, ominous tone. "I've got more battle scars than you can possibly imagine. I'm not a graceful loser, especially when I've already got a thirst for revenge. You don't want to take me on."

Her heart beating fast and furious, she pressed his palm to her breast. Defiantly, she whispered, "I'm taking you on, Aaron. Whatever revenge you've got a taste for, have at it."

Addy had the satisfaction of hearing his strangled groan before he hissed, "Have mercy, woman, I'm only human."

"Then act like it," she said with a quiet confidence. He had called her *woman*, and oh, what a thrill to hear him finally admit it. Almost as thrilling as his hesitant tracing of her breast beneath the aged satin, the way his thumb stroked until she thought she might scream from his taunting.

"You little fool," he whispered roughly. And then his mouth was on hers, consuming as the fires of hell and just as hot. She returned his kiss full measure, refusing to shrink from the fierce avenger she had unleashed. The hunger was in him, she could taste it, could feel it in the clench of his muscles, in the searing power of his raw kiss.

Abruptly, he broke off, and firmly, but with an amazing tenderness, pushed her away. He moved away from her, until he was swallowed by shadows, and she was left alone in the spotlight of the moon.

She heard the groan of the rocker as he sat down.

"Can you see me?" he asked from a nearby corner.

"No. But I know you're there."

"Yes, I'm here . . . watching. Wanting. Imagining. I've done a lot of imagining since you made me want you on a pile of hay in Papa's barn." The thick voice she heard came from a man she had glimpsed but had yet to fully know. He was a dark stranger, seductive in the quiet danger he posed as he asked, "Make it worth my wait?"

"I—I . . . of course. If I knew what you were waiting for."

Cryptically, he answered, "Dreams that are realized, they're never free. A lot of dreams will come true for you, Addy. But till then, make one of mine happen? I'll worry about paying up in the morning."

An alarm, so certain and insistent, it had to be instinct, rang out a warning that the price would not be his alone to pay. So be it, Addy decided. They could make their bed, whether in heaven or hell she didn't care, just so long as they slept in it together.

"Anything for you, Aaron. What do you want me to do?"

"Take off your dress," he said swiftly and just as softly. She heard the low groan of the rocker, a rhythmic pulse that sounded like the intimate creak of a bed. "Just the dress, that's all. Take it off, slow and easy. Whatever is underneath it, leave on."

"But . . . why?" she asked, fingering the first button.

"Because I know a dream when I see one." The rocker creaked slightly faster, as did her hammering heart.

SEVEN

She was a vision. Even from his voyeur's distance, she was a vision wrapped in moonglow, enticing him to join her on the midnight stage. It wasn't that her slow disrobing was marked by the finesse of ease, nothing so familiar as that. It was the way her unmanicured fingers fluttered from button to button; her catching little breaths as she darted a glance from his dark corner back to the task that required all her concentration.

She moved him. With no more than her downward roll of the frayed garters and the serviceable pair of stockings they held up, she moved him. He was humbled by the rare work of art she was, one deserving of tribute. But how could even a master craftsman capture such innocence, pure and delicious, spiked with the seductive allure of a natural temptress?

Raw desire ran through his veins, while his soul reached for hers as if it were a phantom spirit rushing toward its mate. It was a wonderful, horrible sensation. He wanted her too much, and he'd wanted her too long. Yes, yes, it was happening, just as he'd feared, the need that was in him, rising and expanding, crowding out reason and control.

For both their sakes he had to stop this insatiable desire inside him, but how? *How?* How could he not need her bright spirit that lightened the shadows of his own? How could he look at her without aching to touch her, intimate and deep?

He was mesmerized as she drew down a slip strap from her shoulder.

"Leave the other where it is." The urge to rush to her and fell them both to the floor was almost blinding. Somehow he managed a slow, deliberate pace. And then he was there, running a fingertip beneath the thin white fabric that was the only obstacle between her bare breasts and his mouth.

"I love your mouth," he told her while his fingers flirted with sure death.

"Even when it's sassy?" she asked with a nervous little smile.

"Especially then. You've got the kind of mouth that's enough to drive a sane man over the edge." Daring to give her a better glimpse of the danger he posed, Aaron murmured, "Imagine what it does to a man like me, who's questioned his own sanity before."

"Now you're teasing me." She chuckled, and he felt her relax. How safe would she feel, he wondered, if she knew the depth of the troubled waters he fought against, only for Addy, with her dreams and rainbows, to tear at the fragile defenses that kept her protected from him?

"I kid you not," he said somberly. "That thirst for revenge I mentioned starts and ends with you. Ask me why."

Her smile wavered. "Why?"

Dipping his mouth to her ear, he whispered softly, "Because you damn near drove me crazy after that night in the barn. And that is a lot to forgive, especially for a man who was raised on the value of holding a grudge."

He pulled back to look her full in the face, to see if her eyes were wary with the realization that she was in the presence of a man obsessed. But no, her gaze was smoky, her lips curving into a small smile of pleasure and disbelief.

"You have a real strange way of flattering a woman, Aaron. But I am flattered that you'd try to make me feel I could ever drive you crazy. Of course, it's no secret that I've always been crazy for you."

Aaron tapped his lips while he stared at hers. "You have to be crazy to subject yourself to me."

"And just what did you have in mind?"

"Nothing would make me feel better than to drive you insane . . . with pleasure. The kind that you'll never forget. The kind that will spoil you for the touch of another man."

He slid his palm between her legs and found they were more giving and enticing than he'd feared. Up he went, until he cupped her possessively. She was wet as soft, warm rain. Even through her panties he could feel what he did to her. He loved it—the heat in his hand, the warmth of her soul.

"What are you doing to me?" she gasped. Her knees buckled, and she grasped his shoulders to keep from falling.

"Mine," he whispered against her halting little gasps. "Tonight you're mine. But only tonight. I'm doing to you what you do to me every time I even think about you." With an impatient yank he broke the thin strap and peeled down her slip.

Her breasts were perfect and firm, a testimony to her youth.

"If only I were younger," he said in a painful confession. "If only you knew what you were getting into and still wanted me the way I want you. . . . To wake up and see what I'm seeing now and know that what we've got is real enough to last . . ."

"Real," she whimpered. "Nothing seems real, Aaron. I—I'm scared of what you're making me feel. Touch me, shake me, just do something to put me out of this strange misery."

"I'll touch you," he vowed. He licked a finger and stroked a taut rosy nipple. Her sharp sigh brought his mouth down, and he whispered, "Let's see if you taste as good as you look."

Damn. Damn, if she didn't taste better than any woman had a right to, and did she have to smell so uniquely divine? Rainwater and wildflowers. And her hands, pressing him close, urging him to get his fill when he couldn't get enough.

He took her down on the bed. And then he was on her, ravishing her mouth and telling her in breathless whispers all the things he wanted to do.

All the things he could not do.

"Take away this terrible ache," she cried brokenly.

"Here?" he asked, feeling for the fever that he feared would break him before he could appease hers.

"Yes, there. But even worse, here." She pressed her chest so close that he could feel the trip-hammer beat of her heart against his own. "Love me," she begged him, then demanded, "*love me,* as a woman. *A wife.*"

"No," he groaned, the ache in his groin as desperate as the need to convince himself of the rightness of his answer. "You don't want me to love you, not that way." He drew down her thin cotton panties and flung them to the floor. "Ask me for a lover's kiss."

"A kiss. Yes, a kiss. A never-ending kiss . . ."

From her mouth to her breasts he kissed her while his hands made love to her hair. And then he bowed his head and gave homage to that part of her that was his at last, and his alone, if only for the night. Parting the gates, he culled the hidden pearl beyond worth that peaked beneath the tip of his tongue. Never had a woman's cry of his name given him such soulful satisfaction; never had a woman's trembling release vaulted him to an ecstasy that soared beyond the physical.

"Addy," he urgently whispered as he kissed his way up her body, taking his time, savoring every nuance of her skin. By the time he reached her mouth, her breathing was slow and regular.

"Addy," he whispered, stroking her cheek. Protectively, possessively, he gathered her into his arms and considered the impossible situation he was in. Nothing was working out the way he'd planned it. So much for returning here to make amends and do some much-needed emotional housecleaning. He only had himself to blame for getting into this mess and succumbing to his weakness of need. And here he was, still savoring the best sex he'd never had and needing her more than ever.

Could he love her as a woman, a wife? Whatever hope he'd harbored that he could somehow prevent it was rapidly fading. Holding her now, he was aware of an instinct so strong, it was primal, verifying a horrible certainty that he could never give Addy an ordinary love. He'd want to wrap her in a love so complete, it would consume her, swallow up her very breath and devour the elusive free spirit that made her unique.

Madness. He valued his sanity too much to risk letting her get any closer. Once inside his head, she'd be all over his heart. And he'd be all over her the same way—wanting to control, wanting to possess.

He understood too well what would happen. Addy would demand her freedom, and when she did, he'd want to hold her tighter. Insecurity would eat him alive, and he'd take it out on her.

He had to get this marriage annulled—the sooner, the better. Had to get Addy on her own before either of them got too dependent on each other.

But first, he *had* to get out of this bed. Another minute of feeling her leg wedged between his thighs, her head on his chest, and her hair sweeping from his chin to his groin and—

With a muffled groan Aaron summoned every stitch of willpower he had to disentangle Addy from his arms. Carefully, lovingly, he tucked her in and brushed a kiss to her temple.

He stared down at her a long time, remembering the child who had been his special little friend. In his mind he saw the progression of a girl he adored, who sparkled with spirit and intelligence and wit. But then she had grown up and shattered the simplicity that had always defined their relationship.

What that night four years ago had done to him. Everything he had believed about himself had been shaken. He had his share of flaws, but he wasn't a bad person, and he most certainly was *not* a molester of children. So what kind of man could love a child as if she were his own, and then, in the blink of an eye, see her in such a way that he ached to ravish her body?

He had no more perspective on that now than he'd had then. The fact that Addy was no longer a child didn't erase the wrongfulness of that past sin in his heart.

Out of habit he did what he could to work it out of his system and hit the floor. A hundred push-ups and he wasn't even winded. At least he could thank her for keeping him in shape. But no way was he about to thank her for the grinding discomfort that refused to go away.

Settling himself into the rocker, he finally caught a few winks. The sound of a cock crowing brought him upright.

His eyes turned to the bed, and he realized it hadn't been a dream. His heartache just waiting to happen was still there, her arms thrown over her head in absolute trust and vulnerability.

But she'd wake up soon enough.

"Aaron," she murmured, "stop that!" After enjoying a few more licks of her cheek, Addy giggled and swatted at—

A hairy thing that meowed and jumped off her chest, then scooted through the cracked-open bedroom door.

A quick look around alerted her that Aaron wasn't anywhere in sight. The only sign that he'd even been there was the indentation in the next pillow. Addy buried her face in it, inhaling his scent, absorbing what warmth he'd left behind. There wasn't much.

Neither was there much warmth in his gruff "So, you're awake" from the doorway. "I cooked some breakfast. We'll probably have company soon, so you need to hurry up and make yourself decent."

What warmth his voice lacked he more than made up for in his heated gaze. With only his pants on he looked good enough to eat.

"But, Aaron, I'd much rather be indecent." Stretching sinuously, she let the sheet spill down to her waist. It wasn't as if she was showing him something he hadn't already seen, but still she blushed slightly. "Let's forget breakfast and be indecent together." With an intimate little giggle she added, "My, but you *are* a most indecent man. A lover's kiss, indeed. If I'd known what that was,

I would've begged for one in the bushes on the night of our betrothal."

Lifting her left hand, she sighed with wonder at the sight of her ring. Then she beckoned him closer with a murmured "Kiss me again?"

He stared at her hard, then squeezed his eyes shut.

"No time for that, we need to get packed."

"Packed!" Addy forgot the ring along with her modesty and kicked away the sheet. Bounding from the bed, she demanded, "How come?"

Aaron opened his eyes and took a halting step closer. But then she saw his fists clench. He jerked his gaze away. A good minute passed before he spoke, his voice rough. "Because we're leaving."

He turned and left the room.

Scrambling for her clothes, Addy realized all she had was a rumpled wedding dress and a slip with a torn strap. She spied his shirt and put it on. More than necessity, it was a reminder of what they had shared, which Aaron was trying to ignore. Besides, married couples shared all sorts of things, and her husband's shirt seemed a good place to start.

"Smells good."

Aaron looked up from his plate. The sight of Addy with her hair a wild tumble, wearing his shirt open to her breasts, caused the coffee to lodge in his throat. Nearly choking, he thought he might lose what little breakfast he'd been able to get down. But the lurch of his knotted stomach had nothing on the palpitations of his heart when she sauntered over.

And plopped herself in his lap.

Her arms looped around his neck, and she murmured, "The breakfast smells wonderful, but not nearly as good as you."

"Uh . . . ummm . . . Addy—" Aaron shoved back his chair, deposited Addy on it, and began to pace. "We have to talk about last night, put it in its proper perspective."

Addy jumped to her feet and swung him around to face her. Gone was the sweet seductress. Her eyes were blazing, and he saw a spitting kitten who was cat-claw mad.

"How dare you make love to me and then—"

"We did *not* make love," he firmly asserted.

"Then just what *did* we do?"

Sucking in a steadying breath, he replied evenly, "We made a mistake, that's what. Smart people learn from their mistakes; they don't repeat them. *Addy.*"

Looking as if he'd knocked the wind from her, she retaliated with a swing at his jaw. Aaron caught her wrist an inch from her mark and gave her a single, fierce shake.

"Don't you *ever* try that again."

"And if I do, what'll you do, Aaron? Slap me back?"

"I don't hit women," he bit out. Moving toward the bedroom, he threw open the door. "Get dressed," he ordered.

Addy huffed by him with an indignant wrinkle of her nose.

The door slammed in his face. Aaron considered throwing it back open and . . . and what? Having it out?

Something hard smacked the wood. Had the door been open, he would have been nursing a broken nose.

He ground a fist into his palm and went to feed the cat the scraps from two full plates.

Nothing better to do. He was already packed.

EIGHT

"Thanks," he said, breaking the terse silence.

"For what?" Addy quickened her pace.

"For keeping up the front."

"I didn't do it for you," she said stonily. "I did it for me."

Marching ahead through the forest path, she caught a low-hanging tree limb and paused until Aaron was a few steps behind her. Timing it just right, she let go.

"Hey, watch it!" he shouted.

Addy stole a backward glance and saw Aaron drop their belongings to rub his cheek with a wince.

She supposed she should help him out, carry her share of the load, but . . . no. Served him right, the jackass, after what he'd put her through these last few horrible hours.

Saying hurried good-byes to Loretta and the rest of her kin had been bad enough. But even harder than that was playing the part of the blushing bride to the devoted groom Aaron had pretended to be. It was a lie, pure and simple, for the benefit of saving face. And the excuse for their hasty departure Aaron had concocted, that was a lie too.

She had her suspicions what his real reasons were, but it sure as heck wasn't because he couldn't wait another day to show off his new wife to his friends and business buddies.

"Addy, stop!" he yelled. Ignoring him, she kept on going. Two steps later she felt him swing her back with such force that she stumbled and fell into the high grass, bringing him with her.

Addy was momentarily stunned, her breath knocked out from her by his heavy weight. Once his stormy face came into focus, she struggled beneath him to get free, and when that didn't work, she beat at his shoulders.

"Get off me, you big oaf!" she yelled.

"Dammit, quit fighting me!" Aaron grappled with her until he caught her flying fists. Holding them high above her head, he panted harshly. "Do you know how close you came to stepping on that rattler?"

Addy went still. "What rattler?" she said, trying hard to ignore the feel of his body covering hers. "I didn't see a rattler."

"Of course not. How could you, when it was on the ground not five feet away and your nose was ten feet in the air?" He muttered a livid curse.

Her stung pride kept her from saying the right thing.

"Sorry as you must be that you saved me that first time, I can't imagine why you did it a second. Where's your good sense, Aaron? You would've saved yourself the trouble of taking me along, and gotten rid of the wife you're planning to get rid of anyhow. Why didn't you let me get bit?"

He stared at her hard, but his eyes didn't agree with his flippant reply.

"Yeah, well, like they say—fool me once, shame on you; fool me twice, shame on me."

"Shamed, are you? For what? Saving me from a snake or feeling like one yourself for having lain with me and then kicking me out of our wedding bed?" He didn't answer except to shift his gaze to her mouth. Still smarting from his rejection, she taunted him with a lick of her lips. "What's wrong, *baby*, cat got your tongue?"

"No," he said with a maddening calm. "But yours is a bit too sharp."

His mouth came down on hers with a vengeance. It was an angry kiss, from the aggressive sweep of his tongue to the capture of hers when she responded. He held her prisoner with his forceful lips until she whimpered. Easing the pressure, he punished her even more sweetly with the gentle fury of a man impassioned.

It was almost more than she could bear, and certainly more than she could resist, this intensity of raw hunger and combative wrath he poured into an endless kiss.

Realizing she was no match against this, Addy accepted her defeat and twined her legs around his. But when she did he released her wrists. Then his hands were in her hair, sifting and stroking, and he was murmuring, "Damn, don't you *ever* scare me like that again."

He kissed her again, a warm, aching kind of kiss. A desperate kiss full of yearning.

She embraced him and reveled in the silent message his mouth gave away. How she loved the feel of his weight, the touch of his hands, a dark stranger's hands, human and needy, not those of a man she had idolized only for him to fall from grace.

But it was better to know him and touch him this way, to be equals in this man-to-woman give-and-take.

She wanted him to feel her own vulnerability, hold her heart with his hands. She led first one and then the other up to palm her breasts.

For a wonderful moment he did. But then he rolled off her. The hands that had fondled her with such urgency were pressed against his eyes, and he was groaning her name.

She reached for him, but something stopped her.

"We'd best be on our way," she said with what little breath he'd left her. Getting to her feet, Addy offered him her hand.

Aaron hesitantly took it. Then he was standing next to her, their gazes locked.

"Yeah, let's get out of here. If we hurry, we can make up for lost time. The skyline's quite a sight all lit up. But night has a way of softening reality. I want you to see the city before dusk."

"Dusk and dawn, Aaron, they're only the moon and sun turning one cheek to the other."

"Maybe, but be prepared for a different view once you look it full in the face."

"Are you talking about yourself, or the city?"

"Both. Just remember that New York is safe in places and dangerous in others. But no matter where you go, it tends to be overwhelming."

"Even for you, after all the years you've lived there?"

"Sometimes. But the trick is, don't let them outsiders know it." He winked. "Our secret, okay?"

She really liked sharing a secret with Aaron, especially one about himself. She grinned at him. He plucked a twig from her hair and gave her a half-smile. Addy brushed a bit of grass from his shirt.

He moved away to gather the baggage he'd dropped. He was lifting the heaviest bundle when she placed a hand over his.

"Let me help." He stared at their joined hands before he shook his head and gave her the lightest weight of their load. She took it, saying, "Thank you, Aaron, for steering me away from the snake. Again."

"Don't thank me yet. Chances are, you would've been safer with the rattler than you'll be with me. Again."

Aaron hoisted the remainder of their gifts, which far outweighed their skimpy personal effects. She'd left most of her books behind with Loretta. It seemed Jonas had taken to her sister and that Loretta was more than a little smitten herself.

It was with a sense of victory that Addy let Aaron lead the way, falling in step behind him on the narrow path.

Neither said anything for the remainder of the trek, but it was just as well since she had some thinking to do.

As his plane came in sight in a thick grass clearing, a wry smile sparked her lips.

There was a lot to be said for giving in for the sake of a truce she'd decided. After all, it wasn't losing if sizing each other up and joining forces meant emerging as equals—albeit with a wariness of each other.

Better that than waging a bloody battle over what both sides wanted and could share if only they put pride aside.

NINE

"Oh my! Oh my! Sakes alive, oh my!"

Stealing a glance at the passenger's seat, Aaron couldn't subdue his broad smile. It was the most he'd heard out of Addy since he'd announced the sleeping arrangements to his soon-to-be roommate.

Separate beds. A safe distance between them in his own digs that Half-moon Hollow couldn't provide. They'd left the mountains a week early and one night too late. He was already paying the piper for what he wouldn't take back even if he could.

Pointing out the window, he said, "Know what that is?"

"Why . . . why, it's the Statue of Liberty!" Addy held out her arms as if she'd embrace the distant torch. Aaron toyed with the idea of lifting Addy's jaw from her lap and clicking it back in place.

Her excitement was contagious. Watching her made him feel as if he were seeing the awesome sights for the first time himself. He let the moment of shared wonder flow over him, as well as the sense of justification that soothed his conscience.

He *had* done the right thing, and it was a welcome comfort to know that at least this part of his plan was falling into place.

"What's *that*?" Addy exclaimed, pointing out the window.

"Looks like Broadway from here. Tell you what, I'll get some tickets to a play and treat you to a night on the town. Maybe invite a friend or two along to join us."

She turned from the window and gave him a beaming smile. "You've got a lot of friends, I bet."

"I'm not exactly a social animal, but I do have a few."

"If they're your friends, they must be fine folks. I can't wait to meet them! I mean, they're bound to be different from the folks at home."

"You could say that," he said with a laugh.

"And I'm bound to be a lot different from them." There was a sudden anxiety in her voice that made him reach for her hand. Addy squeezed it tight.

"That you are," he agreed. "But that difference will set you apart in a special way. They'll love you, Addy."

"You really think so?" she asked hopefully.

"Take my word for it, you'll be like a breath of fresh air." Just thinking about the crowd sure to vie for her attention had Aaron clenching his jaw. He jerked his hand free.

"Why'd you do that?"

Because you need me for now, and I need you to need me. And that's something I won't outgrow once you outgrow your dependence on me. He forced a tight smile.

"My hand was going to sleep." He shook it and fiddled with the controls. Trying to get his mind off the dreaded inevitable, he made a quick mental tally of what he needed to teach Addy to help her fit in:

All things practical, such as managing money, shopping at the local grocery, how to walk down a street without getting mugged. And of course there were the all-important social nuances. Clothes—now that was a biggie. Restaurant protocol was quite important too. Then there were the finer skills, such as the merits of being discreet in delicate situations. . . . The list went on.

"A crash course with Professor Higgins," he muttered.

"Is that one of your friends?"

"Unfortunately, no." Aaron laughed around a groan. Lord, he hoped she never changed. But she would. And at least for now he was the wise, worldly host and Addy his very own Eliza Doolittle.

"A most astute observation," he said in his best Rex Harrison imitation. Then, unable to resist, he added, "My fair lady."

Addy kissed him soundly on the cheek, with a sigh of delight.

After checking in at the airport, Aaron called a taxi. While they waited, he kept a protective eye on Addy as she wandered about the waiting area, touching this and that.

When she fingered the buttons of a vending machine, he gave her a handful of coins and said, "Dinner's on me."

Plunking in the change, she punched her selection, then clapped her hands when a candy bar rolled out. Quarters and more quarters she plowed with such enthusiasm she could have passed for a slot-machine junkie. With her hands full of junk food, she all but danced her way out when the cab arrived, calling "Howdy!" to the people she passed.

Addy seemed oblivious to their stunned expressions, quickly lowered gazes, and barely muttered hellos. Once the baggage was loaded and she was safely confined to the cab's backseat, Aaron firmly advised her, "From now on you need to save your 'howdys' for people you know."

"But how will I make any friends of my own by being unfriendly?"

"You can worry about making friends after you learn some important rules. Rule one: Don't talk to strangers. Rule two: Don't make eye contact with strangers. Rule three—"

"I don't much care for your rules, Aaron."

"I'm not asking you to like them, just to abide by them."

He tapped the glass separating them from the cabbie. "We're not in Half-moon Hollow, we're in New York. If you're going to live here, then you have to do as New Yorkers do, and that means learning certain rules."

"Seems real sad to me that folks are so scared of each other around here that they don't even smile."

"I suppose it is a bit sad," he agreed. "But that's the way it is."

Rather than argue with him, Addy shrugged. She had better things to do than argue. This cab was so different from the few trucks she'd seen in the hollow. And though she'd ridden in one once, it was closer to a spirited horse compared to this chariot that sped over streets instead of rain-washed dirt and gravel.

A sudden swerve and a honk were followed by the cabbie's middle finger pointing to heaven. Looking in the direction of his cursing yell, Addy saw several—people?—jump up and down while they cupped their mouths to yell back.

"What's the matter with their hair?" she gasped, scooting closer to Aaron. "They look like they've got icicles growing out of their heads! And—and all the rest of it's shaved off. Do they have some sort of mange or a terrible disease?"

"Only if you count bad taste," he replied dryly.

"And the way they're dressed!" she exclaimed, turning to look out the back window. "Look at all those chains! And I could swear those men are wearing lipstick. What ever would possess them to do such a thing?"

She felt Aaron's arm come around her, his light stroke and soft chuckle reassuring.

So many strange-looking people! So *many* people. And buildings reaching so high that she couldn't see the tops, even with her neck arched as far as it would go.

"We're home." Aaron took his arm away to stuff

some bills into the drawer in the window. She was sure it must be enough money to feed a family for a month, but before she could protest, Aaron pulled her out of the cab with him.

She practically had to run to keep up with him as he led her into a big white building. When she hesitated at the door made of crisscrossed steel, he said impatiently, "Get inside, Addy."

She noticed his attention was on a stranger walking real fast their way. When the stranger stopped a few feet from her, Aaron stepped forward. Then the man said, "Hey, mister, spare some change?"

"Get in, dammit," Aaron whispered harshly, nearly shoving her inside before he reached for the bags she'd dropped at the sight of what had to be a beggar.

While Aaron was busy gathering her baggage, Addy gave the beggar the rest of her candy bars from the vending machine.

"Hey, what's this?"

"It's not money, but at least it'll fill you up."

The stranger stared in disbelief at the good fortune in his hands.

Aaron slammed the door, hurried them into the elevator, and punched a button. Lips tight, he bit out, "The rules, Addy, you *have* to learn the rules."

"What's the matter with you?" she shot back. "Leavin' that man with hardly enough food for a skimpy meal after sending that nasty-talking cabdriver off with more money than I've ever seen at one time in my life?"

"The rules," Aaron said again tersely. "Repeat after me: I will *not* talk to strangers."

Holding on to the steel bar edging the lurching cage, she protested, "But he was hungry."

"There's a lot of hungry and homeless people in this city, Addy. Some of them can be dangerous. He could have pulled a knife on us. Or a gun, or—are you listening to me?"

She answered him with a stubborn silence.

"Look . . . I don't want you to get hurt, that's all. Promise me that you won't talk to strangers. Please?"

The fact that he seemed so concerned over her well-being touched her in a way his bullying hadn't.

"Well, all right. I promise. But tell me something, Aaron. What if you knew he was hungry and homeless? Would you have asked him into your home and given him something to eat?"

"Of course not."

"But the Bible says you never know when an angel might appear as a needful stranger at your door. You shouldn't be so hard-hearted."

"It's a hard city," he returned defensively.

"I bet—if everyone's as stingy with their good fortune as you are."

"I am *not* stingy. I contribute to several charities."

"Now you sound more snooty than stingy."

Aaron opened his mouth to defend himself. But then he shut it. *Was* there a certain pompousness in his selective giving? He tried to see it as Addy would and was disconcerted to feel the sting of guilt. Sure, he felt good about helping out a worthy cause. But he felt better about the write-off on his tax return.

He was still mulling over his selective generosity

when the elevator stopped at the top floor. His floor. Somehow it looked different to him as he took in Addy's big eyes and heard her gasp of awe as they came into the entranceway.

"Just look at this fine floor." She dropped to her knees and traced the shining black-and-white tile. "Aaron, I knew you'd done well for yourself, but I had no idea that you lived like this. But . . . don't you need some furniture?"

Tossing down the baggage, he lifted her up and nearly lost himself in her eyes. She was looking from poverty's view at a privileged way of life that he had come to take for granted. He realized that Addy had been right about him hardening his heart.

But staring at Addy's face, he saw the appreciation for a simple loaf of bread, a tin roof over one's head, and a battered pair of ill-fitting shoes. In Half-moon Hollow his life had been privileged compared to hers. Here, it was so beyond comparison that he felt embarrassed by his riches.

Riches that he wanted to lay at her feet.

Feeling proud and yet humbled, Aaron turned her to face the far end of the entry that he knew to be twice the size of the tiny shack that Addy had shared with her family of ten.

Pointing to the glossy white double doors with gleaming brass handles, he said, "Your new home is behind there." He gave her a gentle push. She walked so slowly that even with the load of luggage he had to gather, he beat her to the door.

"Keys," he said, enjoying a ridiculous sense of self-importance as he pulled the key ring from his pocket and unlocked the door.

Watching Addy from the side of his eyes, he threw open the doors and with the press of a switch said, "Let there be light."

Addy blinked. She blinked again. Where *were* they? Her eyes darted from one end to the other of the vast open space. From the floors, so smooth and shiny, to the high vaulted ceiling, to the slight curve of the endless wall, all she could see was white. Stately pillars, all kinds of statues, all shapes and sizes, all of them white.

White sheets were draped over no-telling-what, looking like eerie ghosts. *Everything* was white except for bright splashes of color on the paintings scattered around. Craning her neck, she looked up at the ceiling again.

And then she realized it was only mostly white. A pale blue sky peeked through the clouds that seemed to float overhead. Far into one corner she saw a hazy sun. And far into another was a half-moon.

"What *is* this?" she whispered in awe. "A castle?"

"It's a loft." From behind her Aaron's voice dipped near her ear. "Like it?"

"Like it?" she breathed. "How could you ever bear to leave this fairy-tale palace?"

"I've been known to hibernate for a month at a time. When I do, not even James—my dealer—bothers to call, since I unplug the phone. He's got a vested interest in leaving me alone when the muse strikes. Unfortunately, I'm more comfortable living where I work than I am working where I live these days."

Aaron nudged her forward, but for the life of her, she

couldn't move. And then he did something wonderful. He picked her up and carried her over the threshold in arms so strong that she felt like a cherished, pampered bride.

She couldn't miss his reluctance to put her down. Then he tossed in the rest of their belongings and, with several clicks, locked them in.

"There," he pronounced. "Now that we're safe and sound, time to take a tour. First stop, the kitchen."

While he showed her the various contraptions and how they worked, her gaze kept going to a shiny square box.

"What's that?" she asked, touching a button, then jumping when it let out a high-pitched *beep*!

"This, my dear woman, is the most important invention known to man since electricity." His chest brushed against her back, sending electric sensations down her spine as he opened the small door. "A microwave. Want to try it out?"

At her enthusiastic nod he went to the pantry, then presented her with a heavy little square of paper.

"Popcorn," he said, his hands gently squeezing hers. "You like popcorn, don't you, Addy?"

"Sure." She glanced up at him. "But I like you a whole lot better."

She saw his Adam's apple rise and fall, a welcome assurance that he was more interested in her than the microwave.

"Won't be half as good as fireplace popped," he said hoarsely. "But it is a whole lot quicker. Put the bag in here."

Since he was wedged in a corner, it was too tempting not to lean against him while she did as he directed.

"Next you shut the door. Good." Addy felt his chin nuzzle the top of her head as he pointed to the control panel. "See the word 'popcorn' on the menu? Touch it." She pressed the small button, and then she touched his hand that was clenched on top of the little cooking machine.

"Now what?" she asked with a breathy sigh.

"We wait."

"Like this?"

She felt one broad palm rest on her hip, while the other twined in her hair and pulled her head back. "No. Like this."

His lips brushed one temple, then the other, pausing to kiss each closed eyelid. He made a lazy trek down her nose, but before he reached her eager lips, a shrill *beep* went off.

Aaron slowly set her away. "It's ready and waiting," he murmured. "Go ahead, take it out."

Her gaze instinctively lowered to his trousers. With all sincerity Addy confessed, "I'd love nothing better."

He moved away. "I'll get the bowls, you get the popcorn. And beer, how about a beer, Addy? Wait, you're not legal. I'll drink the beer—both of them—want a soda?" Before she could answer, he slid her a bowl and left the kitchen, calling over his shoulder, "Pizza sounds good to go with that beer. I'll put a movie on the VCR to keep you company while I hit Mario's down the block. Best pizza you'll ever eat."

"I imagine that's a fact since I've never eaten a pizza

before," she called after him. She got the popcorn out of the microwave door, and spent several minutes trying to open the scorching-hot bag before Aaron came back into the kitchen.

"The movie's on. Sit back, relax, make yourself at home. Look around all you like, just don't snoop under anything that's draped. I'll lock up, and don't answer the door if anyone knocks, okay?"

"Okay. Anything else?" she asked hopefully.

"Uh, yeah. If you want to get cleaned up, use the shower, not the Jacuzzi. And don't leave any towels on the floor; that's one of my pet peeves. The only thing worse is panty hose dripping from a shower rod."

Before she could ask him what a Jacuzzi was, Aaron was gone. Addy couldn't deny she felt a bit deserted in her new home. Then again, a part of her was glad that Aaron wasn't there to watch her poke around to her heart's content. Besides, she wanted a beer, legal or not. She was legal enough to toast with a swig of 200-proof moonshine and get married to a man who was as infuriating as he was downright . . . what had he called her on their wedding night? Delicious. Ummm. That he was.

"Thanks for nothing, Aaron," she grumbled while sloughing off her jeans. Deciding he probably wouldn't like them on his kitchen floor any more than he wanted towels lying around the bathroom, she slung them over her shoulder before getting herself a beer.

Two swigs and Addy decided it was weak-livered stuff. Since she was thirsty, she slammed it down, crushed the can, then got herself another.

Strolling toward the sound of voices, she noticed the great room was sectioned off in spaces.

She walked through what must be the parlor area, with a funny-looking couch shaped like a curvaceous woman lounging on her side and several odd-shaped chairs surrounding it.

In the corner was a huge fancy tub that Addy figured was the Jacuzzi. It reminded her a bit of her favorite swimming hole back home, especially with all the green plants growing wild around it.

"And just what might this be?" Addy fingered the hem of a flowing white sheet. She was real curious about what Aaron had hidden under there, but he had told her not to snoop.

She was debating whether or not to let curiosity win out when she heard a *brinng, brinng*. On the third shrill ring she headed for its source.

And heard Aaron's voice.

"If you got the right number, you know who this is. Tell me why you called, and I'll get back with you later."

What a rude greeting, Addy thought, not so much as a howdy or a good-bye. Seemed to her that Aaron had more facets than a quartz crystal, and this one she didn't much care for. But what she heard next, she cared for even less.

"Oh, Aaron, darling," the female's voice crooned, "I know you're gone, but I was sooo lonely in this big bed. Call me the very second you get home, and we'll do dinner, and we can have each other for dessert. I'm *très* horny, lover. So . . . are you hot?"

A wet smacking sound. "Call me, Aaron. Oh, and you'd better know this is Claudia, or you're in deep shit."

Addy stared mutely at the voice box, her unblinking gaze on the flashing red light. Her heart seemed to be everywhere but in her chest, dropping to her feet, bouncing from wall to wall, and pounding against her ears.

But the longer she stared at the blinking red light, the more outraged she became.

The hussy had a name. The Jezebel hussy called herself Claudia. Did she look as cheap as she talked? Never mind she had a voice that dripped with so much culture it was a wonder she didn't drown in it. As for Aaron, if he so much as thought about "doing dinner" with anyone but his wife, he had another think coming.

Try as she might, Addy felt her seething anger give way to a deep hurt and a fear of the ultimate betrayal. She stumbled away from the voice box, a hand to her mouth choking back dry sobs. She headed for the kitchen, telling herself all the way that Aaron was her husband and that she'd never give him up.

But as she cried into her beer with only a movie for company, a terrible realization hit her. Aaron had a life that didn't include her, except for what he was inclined to share.

While she waited and waited, hoping that he'd return any minute, Addy drowned her sorrows and pretended to strangle Claudia with each crush of a can.

TEN

Pounding on the door, Aaron shouted with a slight slur, "Hey, Addy . . . *baby* . . . lemme in!"

No answer. And then he remembered his latest rule: Do *not* open the door. Good girl, he thought.

Aaron dropped the pizza onto the floor and culled his keys. "Oh, honey, I'm ho-ome!" he singsonged, booting the pizza box in with his toe. When Addy didn't answer he sent dinner sailing with a smooth kick worthy of Pele in his prime. The pizza landed inches short of the delectable lump sprawled in front of the big-screen television.

"Hey, babe, it's chow time. Sorry I'm late, but could I interest you in a food truce?"

He was still snickering at his own wit when he stepped on a can. By the time he reached Addy's slumped head, he'd counted nine cans total. One more beer can than he'd slammed down before stumbling home, minus the worry that he was capable of getting it up.

But one look at Addy all sweet and dead asleep and he was left with no doubt that he'd have to be dead before the mere sight of her didn't stir his blood.

Aaron lifted her hand, then let go, grimacing as it slapped the floor. Addy was gone and wasn't coming back unless all that beer decided to come up. The evidence was plain enough. Sure, he'd been a real jerk to leave her stranded in a strange place for two hours. But that wasn't reason enough for her to get herself drunk.

Aaron shook his head in confusion. He picked her up, as well as her discarded jeans, and carried her through two high columns draped with white silk before laying her on a black iron four-poster bed reserved for guests. The temptation to climb in with her was strong, but once there, Aaron knew he'd do more than touch her. He'd stay forever.

Scary stuff. The lust thing, he could vent. One call to Claudia and his baser needs would be seen to. No soulful satisfaction, but it would get him by.

He stroked a fingertip over Addy's cheek, and she sighed his name. His gaze drifted down to her bare legs. And then his hand was suddenly there, too, his palm hovering over a slender thigh. For a moment he allowed himself to absorb the feel of her body's heat.

His palm lowered for a brief caress before he pulled a blanket from the end of the bed and tucked her in. Hastily, he made his way back to the pizza.

In a fit of frustration he tore open the soggy cardboard and chewed a slice with such vengeance, it could have been Addy herself he swallowed.

Aaron patted his stomach and eyed the remaining pieces.

Nah. He'd save them for Addy. She could eat them with his blessing while they walked on eggshells of destructive desire and shared splitting headaches for breakfast.

Where the heck had those drums come from? Addy wondered, covering her ears. But that only made the pounding worse.

Was she dead? If so, she was surely consigned to hell.

But, no, she wasn't lucky enough to be dead, Addy decided, when a distant clanging noise competed with the splitting of her skull.

"Rise and shine, Sleeping Beauty!"

Addy peered from under the pillow she'd pressed over her throbbing head.

"Go. Away." She groaned, pulling the pillow down over her face as Aaron came in with a tray.

It hit the floor like the shot of a gun just before the pillow was wrested from her grip. Aaron plumped it, set it against the headboard, then hoisted her up until her aching head lolled against the downy cushion.

"First course, a double dose of extra-strength Tylenol with an orange-juice chaser."

"I don't want—" Two bitter-tasting pills landed in her open mouth, followed by a glass of freshly squeezed juice.

"Next course, toast." While she chewed dully, Addy eyed the bleary face of her tormentor.

"What time is it?" she muttered after a dry swallow.

"It's close to noon, and we've got a full day ahead of us. I'd like to be out of here in half an hour." He reached down and came up with a plate in one hand, a cup of coffee in the other. "Hungry? Thirsty?"

Addy shook her head.

"I made it just for you," he murmured, passing the steamy scrambled eggs and fried potatoes under her nose.

She didn't have the energy to confront him outright, but Addy was definitely up to fishing. "Do you always serve breakfast in bed to your sleepover guests?"

"No, but I don't usually feed them myself, either, after they refuse to eat what I've cooked." Aaron slid a fork full of fluffy eggs through her lips. Another bite and then another. By the fifth bite she couldn't help but notice he got faster and more generous with each dump of food into her mouth.

Addy held up her hand and garbled, "Enough!" She gratefully accepted the coffee, and after a sip said, "You don't look so good, Aaron."

"If I look half as bad as you, then I must be a sight for sore eyes."

Self-consciously, she raked back the hair that was falling around her shoulders and in her face, then rubbed her own stinging, swollen eyes.

"You really tied one on last night. How come?"

His caring tone chipped away at her wobbly defenses. The horrible answering machine replayed itself in her ears, and her stomach twisted queasily. Her eyes began to sting worse, and she blinked back the tears.

"Who's Claudia?" she asked quietly.

"So that's it." At her stilted nod Aaron blew out a long, low sigh. "Since you heard the message, I think it should be fairly obvious. She's my lover, Addy."

A vision of Aaron sharing with Claudia what he refused to share with her sliced cruelly through her heart. Gripping the blanket, Addy forced herself to ask, "Do you love her?"

"Hell, no!"

Relief, pure and abundant, washed through her like white-water rapids. "Then you won't be seeing her again, right?" When he lowered his gaze and rubbed hard at his temples, she said urgently, "Aaron, tell me you won't be seeing that awful, cheap-talking woman anymore."

"She's not awful. Just . . . shallow."

"No more shallow than you if you're enjoying her favors and sharing yours!"

"That's not true," he was a little too swift to say. "The act itself might be shallow when there's a lack of emotion attached. But that doesn't make a person shallow. Just human and desperate enough to settle for a trade-off of bodies to get through a lonely night."

Her eyes pleading, she said brokenly, "But now that I'm here, you don't have to be lonely, not ever again. And—and you can't deny there's plenty of emotion between us, whether or not we're touching. There's no need for you to turn to another woman again, Aaron. Not now. Not ever."

Aaron opened his arms. "Come here, Addy."

Shrinking away from his offered comfort, she said in

a painful hush, "If you're planning on speaking to that woman again, don't you even try to touch me."

And then Aaron wasn't trying to touch her anymore.

Addy pressed her palms over the physical ache that filled her chest. She blinked back tears she'd strangled on before letting him see. "So, there's my answer?"

"I'm sorry. But yes." At her sharp whimper he hurried to add, "You have to understand something. Claudia and I—"

"I don't want to hear her name coming from your lips," she cried. "Those very lips that were surely kissin' her and put on places I can't bear to think of, while I was waiting and dreaming of you coming back for me."

Aaron shook his head, sadly. "I think, Addy, that it would have been better for us both if I hadn't come back."

To hear him say such a cruel thing was even worse than what she'd already endured. Striking out, she demanded, "Then why did you do it?"

"It's . . . complicated."

"So, you think I'm too simpleminded to understand."

"No, it's not that at all. It's just that—ah, hell. Let's just say that I came back to correct a wrong if I could. Not that I wanted to, but it was either that or kiss my career good-bye. A dry spell is one thing, a drought with no rain in sight is another. I haven't turned out a piece of work I'd consider signing in the last two years."

"I bet," she snapped. "You were probably too busy getting through your lonely nights to have enough strength left to lift a paintbrush or pound a piece of clay."

He flinched before pinning her with a cold glare. "If you must know, it was more like I was so sapped from pounding my fist into wasted clay and throwing half-finished paintings out the window that those lonely nights were all I had to get me through the next empty day."

A part of her sympathized with him, but she couldn't help retaliating.

"I can't help but wonder what Half-moon Hollow had to offer that Claudia couldn't manage."

"Sarcasm doesn't become you, Addy."

"But carrying on with a shallow woman becomes you just fine, I suppose. What *did* the hollow have that she didn't, Aaron? No, don't tell me. Didn't you say you called yourself a primitive artist? I saw that fancy bathroom of yours, and—" She slapped her forehead. "Of course, that's it! Primitive artist that you are, you were sure to get all fired up at the sight of an outhouse and a Sears, Roebuck catalog."

"Guess the folks at home will have to make do with what they've got, since the catalog's gone belly-up." Rising, he said tersely, "As for me, I've had a bellyful of this conversation. Get dressed, and make it fast."

She threw a pillow at his retreating back in frustration. The only sign that he'd so much as felt it was his quick stop and the glare he sent her over his shoulder.

Glaring back, she yelled, "You stop right there, Aaron!" *Ohhh*, that hurt her head. Lowering her voice to a seething whisper, she demanded, "What wrong did you come back to right?"

He took her in from the top of her head to the tip of her toes.

"Simple, Addy. I'd hoped to salve my conscience by bringing you here if you weren't already married. I thought if I gave you the chance you'd begged me for, I could make some kind of peace with myself and with you."

Her stunned silence gave way to a radiant smile. It vanished when Aaron picked up the pillow and threw it hard, sending a vase crashing off the nightstand.

"Some friggin' kind of peace, huh? Well, let me tell you something, lady. Claudia might be shallow, but at least she's safe. And that's a helluva lot more than I can say for you. Now get dressed. We're out of here in ten minutes."

Long after he was gone from sight, Addy rubbed her arms against the bone-cold chill that had settled in. But then her shiver stilled to a warm hum as hope eternal began to flow.

Filled with a certainty of her power, a power that Claudia didn't have, Addy felt more than ever that she and Aaron could be to each other what she'd always dreamed. It was destiny, she knew it.

ELEVEN

"She'll try on that and that. And that." Aaron pointed out the three most savvy-conservative outfits the designer boutique had to offer in Addy's size.

"But I don't like that, that, and that." Examining a frivolous cocktail dress, she said, "I like *this*."

"It's too lacy. Too feminine. We need to give you a certain look that's subtle and a little aloof."

"Why the heck would I want to look like something that I'm not?"

"Because you're no more subtle than you are aloof, that's why. But if you dress like you are, then it'll give you an edge, give others the impression that you're nobody's mark."

"I'm *not* a mark," she informed him indignantly. "And besides that, people can either like me the way I am, or they don't have to like me at all."

Aaron subdued a smile of approval, as well as an

instinctive wince. Leave it to Addy to expose her best qualities while unwittingly pointing out the worst of his.

Running two fingers around the scalloped trim, she sighed with longing. "I've never seen such pretty lace. It's the lace that makes me want this dress." She pressed it to her. "Please? With maple syrup on it?"

Aaron stroked his chin, fully aware that he'd buy out the whole shop for the sweet treat of seeing Addy happy. The problem was, once they were out of here, she'd be dressed for public consumption.

"Tell you what. Try it on, and if it fits, you can have it. On one condition. Everything else is my pick."

"You spoil me." On tiptoe she pecked his cheek, managing to sabotage the fragile distance he'd been able to keep since their earlier clash. "It'll be my pleasure to wear anything you pick, Aaron. Your opinion's the only one that matters to me, besides my own."

Aaron cleared his throat. No help, the thick sensation stayed. "It's my opinion that you'd better go try on that lacy dress." Realizing he must sound as besotted as he felt, he made himself add, "But don't think that I'm spoiling you. After all, when we go out, I can't have my . . ." *Wife*. What *was* he going to call Addy when he introduced her?

"Yes?" she drawled. Her smile could have been the Mona Lisa's—had the Mona Lisa been a vamp.

"Never mind. The point is, I'm seeing to it that you're dressed right until you're on your own. So get in there." He pointed toward the changing area where their personal assistant had disappeared, her arms fully loaded and dollar signs in her sleekly made-up eyes. "Move it, Addy!"

Addy strolled leisurely to the dressing room with a slow sway of her hips. The woman was going to kill him, strangle him on the urgency of his passion, and tear his heart out, while she was at it.

He *had* to call his lawyer, find out if this marriage was even legal, and get it annulled if it was. He had to do it, as he'd sworn to himself he would. Do it, before he lost what sense he had left. Do it, before Addy beat him to it.

"Champagne?"

"Maybe next month. Maybe never," he replied. "A phone. I need to use a phone—in a private office, please."

A few minutes later Aaron returned having set his plan into motion, but he felt none of the relief he'd hoped to feel and felt more guilt than he'd expected. He told himself that he'd done the right thing, only it didn't *feel* right. A sense of dread, and the growing certainty that his decision was impulsive and wrong, caused his insides to knot. But he was committed now, the meeting scheduled for that night.

And then his breath caught. All lace and fine-ness, Addy strolled barefoot onto the stage. Between the flounce of white petticoats and black silk, he decided the designer had a previous life as a cancan dancer. And Addy was sure to make that decadent bit of frivolity the hottest new craze in the Big Apple.

"So? What do you think?"

What he thought was that his phone call had been the

smartest move he could make. Logically. Instinctively? *Stupid!*

"You wear it well," he assured her, getting up from his chair for a closer inspection. Once he reached the small stage, he half listened to the haute couture assistant tick off the merits of the dress and then list the accessories to enhance the total look.

"No," he said, circling Addy. Though she lacked the height and anorexic thinness of a runway model, even standing still, she was a study in uninhibited grace. She was a sculptor's dream, a model to die for.

Addy as model.

Aaron's heart beat faster. His fingers tingled.

"Aaron? Why're you looking at me so funny?" She began to fidget beneath his fascinated scrutiny. "Maybe I should go try on something else, what with time being so short."

"Forget the time." Not taking his eyes off Addy, he gestured impatiently to the assistant. "A ribbon. Red satin. Can you find me one? Take it off something else if you have to, and I'll pay for the whole dress."

"But that's wasteful if the dress doesn't fit," Addy protested. "Besides, I don't feel right about you spending so much money on me as it is."

"Believe me, my money was never better spent."

"But it makes me feel more indebted to you than I already am. The way you've taken me in and fed me and—"

"And you would have done the same for me, for anyone, so enough of that." The assistant returned with the ribbon, and Aaron slid it around Addy's neck, entranced by the contrast of scarlet satin against her sun-kissed skin. The elegance of her throat, the generous hint of breasts rising from the lace edging . . .

His pulse rushed on the hot current of a vision.

"We need a pair of stockings. Let's see, black? No, white. But not opaque . . . fishnet stockings. And a pair of garters—same color as the ribbon. Can you handle it?"

"Certainly, Mr. Breedlove. We have a marvelous selection of intimate apparel and—"

"Then would you have a merry widow? Something delicate, white satin and lace. And pearls. Pearls, it has to have pearls." Assured that anything he could possibly want was his for the asking, he continued to visually strip the dress away.

"Really, Aaron, you're being way too generous. And since I want to pay you back . . ."

He saw her lush sensuality and innate innocence just as he had on their wedding night. And yet, he saw her from a new perspective. Tilt of the lens in his mind's eye, angle of the viewer and . . . there. *There!*

Captured, he had it!

He bowed in silent, humble gratitude at the throne of his muse, returning at Addy's behest. He was hard-pressed not to drop to his knees and kiss her bare feet. And he might have done just that had he not feared he'd work his way up from there.

"Besides what you requested, I brought several other items I thought might suit your particular taste in lingerie," the assistant interrupted.

"We'll take it. Add some extra hose and . . . panties. She needs panties—throw in a few tap pants, the best ones you have. And let's see . . . a bra or two. Robes, nightgowns—" *Teddies.* Better not push it. "Pajamas would be nice. Raw silk. Just be sure everything is the best you've got."

"Should I make the selections for the young lady?"

Young lady? What young lady? And then he realized that she was referring to Addy. Doing a mental double slap, he tried to see her that way. But still, what he saw was a woman so lush and desirable that no male, be he sixteen or sixty, could possibly resist her.

"Go with her, Addy. Pick out whatever you want."

"But what you said about looking a certain way—"

"I take it back. Not for the first time, I'm learning more from you than you could ever learn from me." He gestured to the artful display of clothes. "Go ahead, pick what you want. Don't bother to try anything on, you can model for me tonight—" *Crap*, there it was again, his glaring error. The meeting. "Make that tomorrow. We'll have it delivered then. Too much to take with us to the next stop."

"Where are we headed?"

"You'll see. I'd rather it be a surprise."

"Full of surprises today, aren't you?" A little timidly, she asked, "Would it be all right if I wore this? It's the finest thing I ever put on, except for my wedding dress, and the truth is, I just don't want to take it off."

The thought of Addy wearing her cancan cocktail dress to get her hair shaped—he'd kill Andrew if he took off more than an inch of her crowning glory—was too rich.

"Wear the dress," he told her with a grin. "It'll save us a few minutes anyway. Be sure to get a few pair of shoes. The ones you wore here aren't leaving."

Once they left, he wished he'd supervised the shoe selection at least. Addy's natural grace was hampered by her wobbling attempt to master her first pair of high heels. The high, high heels made her long legs appear several inches longer, but even though the shoes looked great on her, he personally preferred her barefoot or in stockinged feet.

A quick glance at his watch and he knew they didn't have time to walk to their destination in ten minutes, especially with Addy trying to master her new shoes. The problem was getting a taxi.

"Addy, I do believe it's time for your first lesson in hailing a cab. Watch closely while a real pro shows you how it's done." Spying a taxi rounding the corner, Aaron leaned from the sidewalk and extended his arm. "Hell," he muttered when it whizzed by with a honk. When a second taxi appeared, he sprang to the street, waving both hands over his head.

Jumping back from a splash of dirty gutter water, he cursed profusely while the cab veered back into the congested traffic. Aaron guessed that the cabbie almost hit him while trying to get a closer look at Addy. He stole a glance at her himself, wondering if she was more impressed with his proficiency at stringing four-letter words together than she was with his cab hailing.

"They must've already had folks inside," she said. "Thanks for the lesson. Mind if I give it a try myself?"

"Be my guest." Aaron quelled a smirk of only slight

superiority as he pointed to one coming their way. "Better hurry up and start waving," he told her.

Addy promptly lifted a length of starched white petticoat and black satin skirt to reveal a shiny red garter holding up a fishnet stocking. Rather than her arm, she extended her leg. *Scrrreeech*. The taxi stopped so fast that it was nearly rear-ended by the limo behind it.

"Well, I'll be damned," he muttered. And then remembering the movie he'd put on the VCR, he laughed. "*It Happened One Night*. Seems that you learned more from Claudette Colbert than you did from Gable and me put together."

"After you," Addy said graciously, wobbling her way toward the battered rear door. Before she got there, the limo's back window slid down, and the distinguished occupant called out an offer to join him. "Thanks all the same," Addy called back. "But I'm not supposed to ride with strangers!" Then to Aaron, she whispered, "Sorry, I know I'm not supposed to speak to them, either, but I was taught to mind my manners."

Aaron was still smiling when he put his arm around her in the backseat. He felt a fierce pride in the woman by his side.

"You know, Addy," he said, stroking her arm, "no matter what you wear, you always look great. But the way you look now, you could steal away a man's last breath."

"Thank you, Aaron. Sorry about what I said, accusing you of being stingy with your good fortune." Smoothing her skirt, she sighed. "Fact is, you've been so generous that it's going to take me some time before I can pay you back."

"But I don't want you to pay me back. You're an inspiration to me, Addy—and that's worth more than any amount of money."

"Glad to hear it, but I still want to settle my debts."

There it was. Addy's independent streak staring him and his money clip straight in the face, not to mention his heart. Give Addy a shot at minimum wage plus tips in a deli and she'd still have more self-sufficient worth than his hefty Wall Street portfolio could compete with.

Gazing at her while she looked down in wonder at her shoes, Aaron marveled at the magic she'd worked. Pulling her close, Aaron said as casually as he could, "You know, if reimbursing me really means that much to you . . ."

"It does!"

"Then how would you feel about working for me?"

"Cleaning, mending, anything—but I'd do all that for free."

"We can split the chores. But that's not what I had in mind." He tapped his shoe against hers. "I need a model. *You*, to be exact. But I have to warn you that it's hard work."

"Hard work never bothered me," she assured him. Eagerly, she asked, "How do I model? When do we start? And what do—"

Aaron put a finger to her lips, the feel of them tempting him to steal a kiss. "Once we get started, I'll have a hard time stopping. Let's wait till you're settled in. Say, a couple of weeks? If it's a deal—"

She nipped the tip of his finger, then gave him a dizzying kiss. Pulling away, she said breathlessly, "*Deal*."

TWELVE

Addy touched one fancy box after another. The packages scattered over her bed were wrapped in such finery, she hesitated to peel off the ribbons and paper.

"Need some help?" Aaron was leaning against the pillared entrance to her bedroom, watching her.

"Could be. I can hardly bring myself to ruin such a beautiful sight as this."

"But what's inside is even nicer. And besides, another delivery is coming. A little something I ordered for you. Better get started on these if you want mine."

He was spoiling her whether he'd admit it or not. Addy smiled sublimely, the lipstick she'd put on feeling a little naughty on her lips. As for the other makeup, she was still wearing what the store lady had put on for her the day before. She had slept in it, certain she'd never be able to make herself look so wonderful again. She'd slept in her stockings and would have slept in her dress, too, had she not been fearful of smashing the petticoats and creasing the skirt.

Aaron lifted a box and tossed it her way. Her fingers trembling with excitement, she carefully unwrapped it and withdrew a silky green top and matching pants.

"Oh my," Addy sighed, holding them to her. "Think I'll wear this the next time we go out."

"I don't think so. Wearing pajamas on the street is liable to get you the kind of attention I don't want you to have."

Addy laid them in a sweet-smelling drawer, next to her beloved china doll. Reluctantly, she handed Aaron the shirt he'd loaned her, just before he'd gone to meet his business friend James. She had fallen asleep before Aaron got back, but a kiss in the dark seemed more real than dream.

"I guess I won't be needing this, since I've got my own pajamas to wear now. Thank you for the loan, Aaron." When he sniffed at the fabric, Addy hurried to offer, "Want me to wash it? It's all wrinkled up and a bit smelly from all that perfume I put on. Afraid I got carried away, almost bathed myself in the stuff."

Tempted as he was to keep the shirt just so he could sneak a whiff whenever he wanted, Aaron passed it back to Addy instead. "You keep it. Looks a lot better on you than me."

She hugged it to her as if it were a treasure beyond worth. Feeling a need to touch her that he couldn't resist, he took her in his arms, crushing the shirt between them. He was about to throw caution to the wind and kiss her as senseless as she'd rendered him when the buzzer signaling company from below intruded.

"Must be that delivery," he murmured, threading his fingers through the cascade of her hair. "Tell you what." Aaron handed her another package. "I'll answer the door while you tear into this and try on what's inside."

On his way out he glanced back to see the painstaking care she gave to the bow and wrapping, trying to avoid even a tiny rip. His heart softened, yet another sign that he was in deep trouble and there was nothing he could do to stop it. Lord knew he'd done his best the night before. But his inability to carry through with his plan of defense had left him facing the terrible, unavoidable fact:

He was falling, head over heels, and faster than an avalanche. He was a goner, pure and simple, and fate was making him pay.

With an agitated stride to the intercom, he said shortly, "Come." He didn't wait for a reply from the delivery person, who had a lousy sense of timing. Aaron had the locks undone when a brisk rap sounded. Ready to sign for the package, shell out a tip, and pick up where he'd left off with Addy, Aaron threw open the door.

"Claudia."

Before he could utter another word, she breezed inside and began to slither out of the sexy minidress she had on. The zipper slid past her breasts and was close to clearing her navel before he gripped her wrist to stop her.

"Never mind the zipper. Go ahead, tear it off. You know I love it when you get rough." He jerked the zipper upward, ignoring her protests. In retaliation, she gave his shirt a fierce yank, rending the fabric and sending the buttons flying.

"Heavens, but I've never seen so many zippers on a dress before. So, what do you think . . . Aaron? Aaron! Who's—what's—"

"Go on back, Addy." Pushing Claudia's hands away from the fly of his jeans, he nudged her aside when more than anything he wanted to throw her out the still-open door. "That looks great, just—just great. Try on something else while I take care of this . . . this—"

"And just what is *this*?" Claudia nodded in Addy's direction. Addy was making a wobbly beeline toward them in her high heels and zipped-to-the-nines dress with a look of rage, disbelief, and horror.

Addy didn't see the pleading apology of his own gaze. She was too busy glaring at Claudia, who walked around her with a sniff of superior disdain.

"Really, Aaron, if you had to have some variety in bed, couldn't you at least show good taste? All that perfume! Why, the girl veritably reeks. A *girl*, Aaron. Take off the makeup and what is she, maybe seventeen?"

Addy's hands balled into fists. Fearful that she'd take a swing, Aaron hurried to intrude.

"Addy. Claudia. I can explain—"

"So *that's* who you are. Should've known it from your foul mouth." Pushing past Aaron, Addy nearly jabbed her finger into Claudia's chest. "Not that it's any of your business, but I'm eighteen, you—you glossy bit of a magazine ad!"

It was almost worth the awful scene to see Claudia's haughty composure disintegrate to a mouth-agape stutter.

"Who—who in the world *is* she? Or—or should I say, *what* is she?"

"His *wife*, that's what I am. And if I ever catch you putting your hands on *my husband* again, I'll whack those painted fingers off with a whittlin' knife, hook 'em on a casting line, and throw away whatever they catch. Sure to be bad eatin', considering the bait."

Wedging himself between Addy and Claudia, Aaron said as calmly as he could, "I think you'd better leave, Claudia."

"Is it true?" she gasped. "Everything you said last night, that—that outrageous story you told me about growing up in some backwoods town and . . . No, I still don't believe it. You knew I couldn't settle for a kiss, that I'd be back today. And so—so you hired this actress for kicks. Okay, I'm laughing. Ha-ha. Joke's over, Aaron. Pay her off and get this horrid creature out of here."

"The only horrid creature who's leaving is *you*." Addy grabbed his left hand and shoved the timeworn gold band under Claudia's nose. "Until this is off, you have no place here, and it won't be in your lifetime, you cheap hussy." Having backed Claudia to the door, Addy said in a seething whisper, "Aaron, if you've got any more to say to her, you'd better say it now."

Aaron knew he should demand that Addy leave the room so he could end his affair with Claudia with as much grace as he could salvage. But he didn't think he could summon the authority, given that he was stifling a perverse urge to grin at the dressing-down Addy had given Claudia—whose worst trait was a tendency to talk down to others.

Aaron put his arm around Addy. Her chin notched up with unmistakable triumph, but he could feel her spine stiffen.

"I tried to explain last night, Claudia, but you were laughing too hard to take me seriously. I'm really sorry this is the way things had to end. If you want to talk—"

"*Talk*. Talk! I don't ever want to see your face again. My purse?"

Aaron had no sooner pitched it to her than Addy sniffed, "By the way, I might reek of perfume, but your manners stink worse than a skunk liftin' its tail downwind."

She softly shut the door in Claudia's outraged face. All was silent for a good half minute, except for the sound of Claudia's Gucci shoes stomping away. And then, silence. *Real* silence. The kind of absolute quiet that magnified the sound of breathing and the pound of dread that echoed in his head.

Addy threw off his arm and faced him squarely.

"You lied to me." Her whisper was somehow worse than a scream. And then she did—scream. "Lied to me! You said you were going to meet with James on business, but all the while you were with her. *Her!* 'Couldn't settle for a kiss,' that's what she said. So you were kissing her too!"

"One kiss, Addy, a good-bye kiss. I swear, nothing more."

"Nothing more," she spat. "Oh, there was more all right. Why, her eyes turned big as turkey platters when she got a gander at that ring. You took it off, didn't you? Why, Aaron? So she wouldn't know you were married? Or was it so you'd feel less like a cheat?"

He had felt like a cheat. And as if he'd been truly married, he'd tried to salve his conscience with the buying of a gift. He reached for Addy, hoping that a touch might convey his tangled emotions, the deep regret he was feeling. A touch. Lord, but he needed, craved, her touch.

She slapped away his hands and raised both her fists as if ready to pummel him.

"I don't want that woman's leftovers."

"But, Addy, she was the one getting leftovers. Not you." She eyed him with disbelief, as he continued urgently, "It's true. Claudia's a beautiful woman on the outside, but there's not much where it really counts. Why do you think I'd sleep with someone like that when there are plenty of women with substance, who have a lot going for them outside of a bed?"

Addy's glower wavered. She shook her head. "I have no idea, Aaron. But I would surely like to know."

His stomach rolled over. Dear heaven but this was one confession he didn't want to make. Feeling as if he were laying himself down in an open grave and watching the first shovel of dirt head toward his face, he shut his eyes.

"The reason is, I don't like to hurt people—especially those who deserve respect, fair treatment in a relationship. But I couldn't hurt Claudia any more than she could hurt me. She lacks depth of character and emotion. As for me . . ." Eyes open, he let Addy see him as only she could. "I didn't have enough inside me for the kind of woman who was worthy of a commitment, so I settled for someone who had no more to give than I did. My own emotions, they went too deep elsewhere."

A look of surprise and hope filled Addy's eyes. "Where was the elsewhere, Aaron?"

He took her hand and met no resistance as he placed it firmly over his heart. "I'm looking at her right now. The leftovers, Addy, were yours."

Her beaming smile all but knocked the wind out of him; her kittenish lick to his chest knocked it out completely.

"I'm feeling awfully hungry. You don't mind if I help myself to the leftovers, too, do you?"

Aaron took a bracing breath. "Yes, Addy, I'm afraid that I do mind. It's the reason that I tried to call my lawyer, and when I couldn't bring myself to do it, I rang Claudia. When I went to her last night, it was with the intention of getting you out of my system. That's something you deserve to know."

"You—you mean that you set out to betray me?"

"No. No, never that. I was simply trying to save myself from you—for all the good it did."

"But why? *Why*, Aaron? What did I ever say, ever do, to make you think you might need to save yourself from me? Surely, you know that I would never, ever, hurt you."

"Not deliberately, Addy. There's no meanness of heart in you—but you do have a thirst for life. It's one of the most wonderful things about you, and I'd be the last person to ever want to rob you of that. If I could give you the world on a platter, I would."

"But you have." She gestured to their surroundings. "Just look at the home you've given me." Clenching her dress, she said gratefully, "And these clothes. You've dressed me in such finery that I feel as if I've been wrapped in angel's raiment from my head to my feet."

"And you'll be standing on your own two feet without me before too long." When she opened her mouth to speak, he put a finger to her lips. "No, you have to listen to me. I know what I'm talking about because I've been where you are now and where you're sure to go. You're going places. You have the smarts, the personality, the natural ambition and talent to make your mark and carve your niche in life. And you will, Addy. You will, and you'll do it without me. I'm the means to your new beginning, but you won't need me in the end."

"That's not true, not true at all!" She gripped either side of his torn shirt and pulled down, bringing his mouth within kissing distance of hers. "I need you now, Aaron. And I'll need you then," she whispered, urgently. "Any place I ever go in my life won't mean anything to me without you. You're like a rock—"

"And you're like a rainbow. Even if I was foolish enough to reach so long and high that I managed to touch all your colors, I couldn't hang on. As rainbows always do, you'll disappear and leave me with nothing but a memory of what I had and lost. *Memories*, they're as seductive as they are destructive. That's something I learned from you, and I learned it well. The last thing I need is more damage to deal with than what I've already got. That's why I have to hang on to what's left of my heart."

He pushed his hips forward. "As you can feel for yourself, I want you more than anything I've ever wanted in my life. But my life, Addy, such as it is, can't afford an impossible dream. You might be hungry, but I'm past famished. We're not talking a healthy relationship here."

Addy continued to grip his shirt as she carefully considered his words.

"Seems to me, Aaron, that we're on opposite sides of the same fence. I won't give up."

"I know that. And truth is, I'd be deeply disappointed if you did. Love can be a battlefield, Addy. I'm afraid that it won't be long before one of us draws first blood."

"Well, who knows . . ." She slid a fingertip down his chest, past his fly, then dipped to cup him. With a gentle squeeze she murmured, "Who knows, Aaron, it could be you who draws first blood. That is quite a weapon you've got there."

His gaze narrowed, and she felt the sudden slide of his hand up her dress. He deftly slipped a finger beneath the crotch of her panties and swiftly glided it just inside her.

"Yes, Addy, it is. And it's one weapon that I definitely know how to use." He flexed his finger. She drew in a sharp breath—and tightened her hold.

"Funny thing about weapons, Aaron. What matters in the end isn't the owner, it's the person who's handling it."

"That's true," he conceded. "But whoever's handling it better make sure they know what they've got. So . . . go ahead, take it out. See just what it is that you're asking to handle." His upper lip lifted in a sexy taunt, goading her to meet his challenge.

Holding his gaze, she unsnapped his jeans. Her hand slightly trembled as she unzipped them . . . and realized that he had nothing on underneath. His lips tightened while she fumbled to pull out what was proving to be a considerable length. Slowly, her eyes lowered to the weight in her hand.

"*Mercy*," she breathed.

Heart in her throat, she wrapped her palm around him and gave a tentative stroke. In amazement she felt, she *saw*, him grow even larger, and she instinctively clenched inside. Aaron's low chuckle was dangerously dark, infinitely pleased.

"Do you like it? The way it looks, the way it feels?"

"I . . . do," she said, and with a good measure of respect.

"Yes, I believe that you do," he murmured, easily deepening his intimate touch. "Just imagine what it would feel like, look like, moving in and out of you."

Her swallow was drier than dust. "I fear that you could hurt me," she admitted.

"Could I? Oh, yes," he assured her. But then she felt his tender kiss to her forehead. "But I wouldn't if there was any way that I could help it. Hurting you, Addy, is something that I never want to do. Not physically, not in any other way. And I know you return that feeling. But the fact remains that you *will* hurt me eventually. Wounded people are dangerous people. They strike back with any weapon they have. With words, with deeds. Even with their bodies." He paused, placing his hand over hers. "I think you've handled it enough."

When she hesitated, Aaron stopped his fondling. She clamped her thighs, unwilling to give up his hand and refusing to let go of what she held in hers.

"It's wrong to ever use sex as a weapon," she said with quiet conviction.

"Very wrong," he agreed, his breath catching as she tightened her hold. "But that doesn't keep people from doing it. It's exactly what you're doing now."

"That's not true. There's nothing wrong with a touch from someone wanting to give." To prove it, she stroked him with a loving caress. His hips jerked. She opened her thighs, giving him access to her own vulnerability. He took it, exploring her with a stunning sensitivity, fingers like a brush swirling into a last precious drop of paint.

His gaze locked with hers, and she realized that they were engaged in a battle after all. In his eyes she saw an accusation for the damage he claimed she had done to him, for the future hurt he was sure she would inflict. Her own eyes were filled with an assurance that she had never meant him any harm, and his heart would always be safe with her.

One war rolled into another, an intimate crossing of wills as each tried to undo the other. He matched her escalating strokes, swiftly and aggressively plundering her willing body.

Her keening wail of ecstasy's defeat mingled with his gnashing groans as he surrendered to a rampant release.

For a while all was silent except for the sounds of their racing breaths. And still they stared at each other, sharing more than words could ever say. He was shaken but no more than she by the force of a passion so intense, it held the power to deliver or destroy.

How he wanted to sweep her into his arms, carry her to bed, all the while kissing her, telling her that his love was hers, only hers, and it was for keeps. But Aaron knew what folly that would be. If he did, she would profess the same, and he would try to hold her to it, through guilt, control, sex, any weapon he had, when she no longer loved him that way. It was a struggle, but he managed to love her enough not to tell her that he did.

Instead, he withdrew his hand. He held it up between them, making sure that she saw the evidence of her desire.

"First blood has been drawn," he said somberly. "You're a fierce and worthy opponent, Addy. As I said, love can be a battlefield. Consider the war started."

Aaron made a quick adjustment before zipping up his jeans. Then he gripped her shoulders tightly and lowered his face to hers. "Be careful, very careful," he said with the graveness of a final warning. "Desire can be dangerous, especially when it cuts both ways. If you climb into my bed once, just once, you'll have to fight me tooth and nail to ever get out. Think long and hard about it, because if that's your choice, there will be no going back."

He let her go and stepped away. Frowning, she did the same. And then she turned. She was at the front door when he raced after her, calling, "Where do you think you're going?"

"To think." She made her way into the entry and had reached the elevator before he caught up.

Aaron grabbed her hand away from the button before she could push it. "You can't go out by yourself!"

"Of course I can. And I am."

"No, you're not. What if you get lost?"

"I'll ask for directions."

"That's the craziest thing you could do. The only thing worse than getting lost is letting someone know that you are." He was about to berate her for her foolishness when the distant sound of the buzzer went off. *The package.* "Stay right where you are. Don't move," he ordered her, backing away without taking his eyes off her until he darted inside, hit a button to allow the messenger in, and dashed back.

Thank God she was still there. Deciding that his present would be a good peace offering to waylay the brewing fight, he said, "Tell you what, if you still want to go out after I take care of this, I'll go with you. Just give me enough time to change, and we'll get something to eat. Then I'll give you my surprise."

"Why, Aaron, don't tell me that you're planning to give me another bed to keep me out of yours. Not only is it a lot to carry, but the one I've got is fine—even if it gets a bit lonely."

Before he could defend his protective reasoning, the elevator doors opened.

"Mr. Breedlove?" the delivery person asked, discreetly dividing his attention from Addy to Aaron's torn shirt. At Aaron's acknowledgment the man politely asked for some identification. Considering the value of the small parcel from Cartier, it wasn't an unreasonable request.

"Hang on while I get it. Addy? You stay put. I *mean* it." He got his wallet in a flash but stopped long enough to throw on a fresh shirt. When he got back, she was gone.

"Where'd she go?" he demanded.

"Mr. Breedlove, I'm sure that I don't know."

He'd never moved so fast in his life. He flipped out the I.D., grabbed the gift, got into the elevator, and, as the doors were closing, said, "Flip the dead bolt for me, okay?"

By the time Aaron hit the street, his heart was hammering. Frantically, he looked one way and then the other. No sign of her. But then, across the street, he glimpsed the swish of ebony hair as she looked up at the sky. She raised her arms as if she were taking flight.

Aaron all but flew himself. He was nearly run over twice before he gained the dubious safety of the opposite sidewalk. His gaze zeroed in on Addy, who was well on her way, waving at the strangers she passed.

THIRTEEN

The feeling that she was being followed was like an irksome tap on her shoulder. She stopped several times to look behind her, but she didn't see Aaron. All she saw were lots of people, most of them so interesting to look at that she was hard-pressed not to gawk.

But since she didn't want to be rude, she gawked to her heart's content at the variety of store-window displays instead. She was especially taken with the beautiful men and women standing in their Sunday-best clothes. Not so much as a blink, they stared straight ahead. How did they do it? she wondered.

She'd sure like to get a few pointers since Aaron had said she'd have to keep just as still when she started her new job as his model. Looking closer, she decided these models didn't quite look real. While she was trying to figure that out, a young man about her age came out of the store.

"You should try that outfit on. It'd look lots better on you than it does the mannequin."

She took in the spiffy neatness of his black sleeveless sweatshirt that showed off his muscles and his baggy black trousers that matched. He was awfully cute, but it was the earring dangling from one of his ears and his shiny dark shoulder-length hair that really caught her attention.

Curiosity got the better of her. "Who are you?"

"Call me lucky. I work here, but I just clocked out. If you want to try on the outfit, I just clocked back in."

"Howdy, Lucky. I'm Addy." Gesturing to the thing he'd called a mannequin, she asked, "Is it real?"

He laughed. "No. Are *you*?"

"Real as they come." With a sigh she said, "Much as I like those fancy clothes, there's no use in me trying them on. I don't have any money." A tantalizing aroma wafted to her nose. Addy sniffed. "Too bad too. Whatever I'm smelling sure smells good." Her stomach growled loudly. Embarrassed, she explained, "It's been a while since I ate."

"In that case let's get something to eat. My treat."

Addy hesitated. If she wasn't supposed to talk to strangers, she surely wasn't supposed to eat with them. But this Lucky fellow seemed real nice.

"Well . . . sure. But I want to pay you back. And I will as soon as I get my advance." Addy grimaced. Despite her protests, Aaron had insisted that he give her a monthly allowance so she could learn to manage money. The way she figured, it was just debt piling on top of debt, and she'd die of old age before she got it paid off.

"Tell you what. Once you get your advance, you can take me out, and we'll call it even. If you don't mind me asking, what kind of work do you do?"

"I've got a modeling job. But singing's what I do best."

"Really? Say, if you're any good, I've got a friend who's a bouncer at an uptown club. It's more swank than cool, but the owner's always looking for fresh talent."

Addy was fairly certain that Aaron wouldn't look kindly on her quitting the modeling job to sing in a tavern. But it wasn't a bad idea to keep her options open, just in case he fired her.

"Why don't you tell me more about it while we share supper?" She shifted on her high heels. "Could we make it somewhere close by? I need to sit awhile, Lucky."

"My real name's Thomas." He lightly took her arm and led the way. "But my friends call me Tony."

"Pleased to meet you, Tony." Beaming at him, she added, "Guess you could call me lucky now. You're the first friend I've made here."

His heart was racing, his breath hard to catch. But it wasn't from his marathon sprint to beat Addy home by a hair. Aaron took refuge in the cozy clutter of his studio. Wanting to appear busy, he grabbed a paintbrush and cursed softly at the sight of it shaking with the pumping emotions he was struggling to contain.

He heard the front door close, then the *tap-tap* sound of her heels against the floor.

"Aaron?" she called with a hesitance he couldn't miss.

"Yeah, in here," he shouted back. He threw down the brush and smacked his fist into a mound of clay. Digging his fingers into it, he pretended it was Tony Delgado he was choking. Twenty years old, a wannabe actor who landed the occasional bit part. He wasn't a druggie, no known association with any gangs. The manager had believed him to be perfectly safe, and thanks to a twenty-dollar bill Aaron's inquisitive visit while Addy was at an outdoor café a block away would remain a secret.

"What are you doing?" she asked, plopping on a nearby chaise longue.

Aaron quelled the urge to shout, "I'm trying not to puke up my guts, that's what!"

Instead, he managed to say evenly, "I'm thinking. The same thing you said you were going to do just before you took off without me. You've been gone three hours, long enough to chew on your food for thought. So, how'd it go?"

His back to her, he heard the drop of her shoes. A moment later he felt the touch of her palm on his shoulder. With great effort he continued to ply the clay rather than grip her hand and assure himself that her ring was still there.

"I love you, Aaron," she said softly. "And I still want to share your bed something fierce. But . . . I've decided that as usual, you're right. I need to learn to stand on my own two feet before I sleep with a man who's already standing firm on his own."

Fortunately, he was sitting, else his knees would have hit the floor. Damning himself for relinquishing the surest means he had to keep Addy with him, he shut his eyes and asked, "And what made you come to that decision?"

"Let's just say that I realized how far I have to go to understand your way of life. I've got no money, no job other than the one you've given me, nothing that I can call my own. You deserve better than that, and so do I. You deserve a woman who's got as much to offer as you do. And I need a man I feel equal with, not forever and a day indebted to."

She owed him nothing, not even her presence that he was desperate to keep. But he knew that was a moot argument when her need for independence was an irrevocable fact.

"I see," he said, his voice sounding to him as if it came from the depths of a deep dark well. Addy seemed even farther away, though she stood so close he could feel her body's heat. He envisioned her in the future, on her own and holding court with a thousand Tonys who elbowed him out of the way and onto the fringes, where he impotently watched, frantically trying to jockey for a place in her life.

"You don't sound too happy about it, Aaron. Why not? After all, I just came to see things your way."

"Yes, you did, Addy," he replied curtly. "Never mind me, I'm in a funk over this stupid piece of clay." Releasing his frustration, he picked it up and threw it against the wall.

"Want to talk about it?" she asked with such caring sympathy that it made him want to cringe and cling to her at the same time.

"I don't talk about my art with anyone except James. And not even with him lately."

"But why not?"

"Because he doesn't approve of what he considers to be my professional suicide. As for anyone else, my work is too personal to share. I'd feel less exposed if I paraded naked down Wall Street in rush-hour traffic."

"But since I've more or less seen you naked, what would be the harm in sharing your work with me? After all, I am going to be your model, and you did say I was going to have to shed a few clothes myself."

Aaron debated. To make her an intimate part of his artistic dilemma would be to give her access to his most private reaches. And yet he knew he could trust her more than anyone else in the secret world he inhabited, a place where he'd been groping blindly without a leg to stand on for over two years. Until yesterday, that is, when his elusive muse had taken the form of Addy in a ridiculously frilly cancan dress.

"I haven't had a showing for some time," he heard himself say. Feeling a slight lift of the heavy weight he was weary of carrying, Aaron rushed on. "I've got commissions up to my neck that I haven't been able to make good on because that's not where my head or my heart's been or where it promises to be ever again."

"If it's not there, where is it?"

"In a very dicey place." Turning, he met Addy's gaze and saw . . . encouragement, unstinting support.

"Wherever your heart is, it's bound to be good. Don't let anyone ever tell you otherwise."

"The real otherwise is, Addy, I'd be a starving artist all over again if I hadn't invested my money wisely. For me to desert the collectors and critics who've compared me to Grandma Moses while I go in search of the sensual is worse than unforgivable, professionally speaking. Nudes are a hard sell. It doesn't matter if the face is as honest and emotionally bare as the physical poetry of the body."

"You mean that you're wanting to carve out folks, like those statues you've got prancing naked about the house?"

"Yes, but it doesn't end there. I've been experimenting with a concept that merges sculpture with framed pictorials." At her confused expression he went to a sheet spanning nearly six feet that was at eye level on the wall. He prepared himself for the wince sure to follow and took it off.

Addy gasped in delight. "Why, it's like a life-sized person living inside a picture frame!"

"Three-dimensional, like a person, but very light—a reverse mold cast in resin—I carved the frame and had the foundry cast it as part of the whole. This was my first attempt. I'm afraid it's not very good."

"Not good? Aaron, it's beautiful. Wonderful! That woman looks so real, even more real than a mannequin." He noticed that she bit her lip before rushing to ask, "How did you make her skin look like that, waterfall white and smoother than vanilla ice cream?"

"Bonded sand. Not that I know why I went to the trouble to airbrush the thing, other than the fact that I like to finish what I start, even if it's crap."

"Who is she?"

Obviously, he hadn't done even a halfway-decent job. Then again, the model had only vaguely resembled Addy. The spirit he longed to capture was inimitable and residing many miles away.

Aaron shrugged. "No one, really, just a model I hired."

"And she took her clothes off for pay?"

Did he perceive a note of jealousy? Sensing an opportunity, he turned the point back to Addy. "You agreed to model however I needed you to. If I asked you to pose nude, would you do it? With pay, of course."

Addy paused. Then said with conviction, "I'd feel a bit self-conscious, but if that's what you needed me to do, I would right here and now. *Without* pay."

Patting the small package in his pants pocket, Aaron said with a smile, "I'm suddenly feeling hungry. Why don't we pick up this conversation over stuffed mushrooms and lobster with enough drawn butter for a heart attack?"

Addy looked down at her stomach with an expression that indicated she was stuffed.

Rather than make her suffer, Aaron decided to hedge his bets by making Tony's company seem boring in comparison.

"If you can hold off for a while, so can I," he hastened to add. "We could take in a couple of local galleries, maybe even a movie or a game of pool first. . . ." Definitely pool, he was good at that. "So, is it a date?"

Addy looked at him the way she had as a little girl, as if he'd hung the moon and the stars. But best of all, she looked at him as if he were a desirable man she longed to explore until she knew him through and through.

"I'd be honored to go out with you. You're more than a gentleman, Aaron, more than a most wonderful friend. You're a—a genius!"

A genius? "I'm no more a genius than a hero. You, however, are more priceless than a treasure chest filled with every rare stone imaginable."

"But I'm so rough around the edges, Aaron. I don't blame you a bit for wanting to look but not touch."

He shook his head and laughed to keep from crying. "Those rough edges are what make you the prize that you are. See yourself through my eyes. You are a woman beyond worth."

"And you are a prince because you make me feel like it."

"My lady?" He offered her his arm. Her fingers felt like bolts of lightning latching on as she replied, "Lead the way, and I'll follow as if you're the bread crumbs Hansel and Gretel left behind to find their way back home."

"Follow with care, Addy. This is one home that's got a fire in the hearth that makes that storybook witch look like a child playing with matches."

"I'll take my chances." Slanting her gaze up to his, Addy gave him a kittenish grin. "I can imagine a much worse fate than getting eaten alive by you."

FOURTEEN

Addy surveyed her image in the long oval mirror that swiveled on a carved piece of wood in her bedroom. She turned this way and that, frankly admiring herself in her slinky red dress since she wasn't worried about Aaron catching her. He didn't go past her white pillars any more than she did his at the far end of their shared living quarters.

Even when she was naked before him, he did not touch her in the intimate way. Work was work according to Aaron, and though he was a very demanding employer, he treated her with professional respect. It amazed her how exhausting it was to hold a pose, but at least it gave her time to think about all the changes going on in her life.

Little by little, their relationship had changed by leaps and bounds in the last two months. She thought it odd that while their physical intimacy didn't extend beyond kisses, they seemed to be more intimate than lovers in a way. She could read which of his many moods Aaron was in, simply by his expression. He shared his self-doubts when the work didn't go well, his thanks for helping him to accept the roots in which they were grounded. When she offered comfort or support, he took it, and returned the same to her ten times over. But still, there was something that separated them.

He took her into his confidence, even expressing his ongoing worry that while they were closer than close, he was sure to lose her. She supposed that was one reason she didn't confide in Aaron about the circle of friends she had made outside of him. He'd warned her never to be out after dark without him, but from Saturday morning to dusk, her time was her time, and he asked no questions about how she spent it.

Yet more often than not, she had that niggling feeling that Aaron was following her when she was with Tony and the friends he'd shared with her. They were a mite strange but no stranger than she seemed to be to them. She had laughed at them when they tried to imitate her hoedown dance steps. They had laughed at her when she asked them what "rap" was and gagged at her professed longing to wring a chicken's neck and cook up a kettle of soup that didn't come out of a can.

She felt as if she were living two lives. No, three. There was the one she'd been born with and couldn't shake, and the one she had found with her new friends. And then, then there was Aaron's world, a life so vast she couldn't grasp it, yet so fragile she could pop it easy as a bubble with a single wrinkle of her nose. She didn't shake her head anymore, knowing that he'd toss out a full day's work if she did.

Why her opinion mattered so much to him, she had no idea. All she knew was that the longer she knew Aaron, the more interesting he got. Good thing that he was paying her so much. Her debt was decreasing faster than the allowance she was saving—with interest. The sooner she got rid of that stone around her neck, the sooner she could stand on her own two feet, climb into his bed, and be his wife in every way.

If only she could figure out a way to take on that singing job she'd been offered at the club where Tony's bouncer friend worked—

"Lady in red, you are dressed to kill tonight. Can't wait to show you off on my arm."

She jumped when Aaron caught her in her guilty musings. Then, remembering what she'd learned from watching the cultured people in the museums and restaurants Aaron took her to—as well as those rich and famous folks on the *Lifestyle* show—she mimicked their posture that Aaron called poise. She stuck her nose in the air, swiveled around, and—

Melted. *Lands alive!* What she saw was a breathtaking sight. From the toes of his shiny black shoes, and fancy black pants to the white shirt with pleats and a black coat with tails, he was perfect. And what a comely pleated belt, made of deep red satin, with a bow tie to match. And was that a little diamond he had on his ear? It was! And he had a red rosebud on his coat, and a black silk hat. Set at a jaunty angle, he looked to be seven feet tall.

He tipped it with a white-gloved hand. In the other he had a black cane with a gold wolf's head perched on top.

"Mind if I come get a closer look?"

"Why—why, sure. After all, it is your home."

"Your home too, Addy," he insisted. He pitched the cane to the bed. "That's for beating away all the men who'll be trying to steal my girl."

His hands on her bare shoulders, he turned her so that she again faced the mirror. The scent of him, so special and familiar, made her feel a little dizzy. It was the same scent that had intrigued and delighted her senses on a pile of hay in his papa's barn. Then, as now, what she inhaled brought images of black magic, whispered secrets, and rumpled sheets.

"You smell good, Aaron," she said, breathing him in.

"And you smell witchy and sweet." He dipped his head to her neck, and the brush of his nose sent tingling prickles racing through her. "Too good for your own good."

His hands, so large and sensitive, lightly stroked her arms, then raised her palm to his lips. For such a tender, innocent kiss it felt awfully hungry. And possessive.

"Never cut your hair," he murmured, sounding as if it was his and not hers to do with as she pleased. "I always love your hair, but tonight it's even more to my liking. All of it tossed over one shoulder, leaves the other one easier to kiss." He kissed her there, and then said, "Your back's begging for one too. Right about . . . there. And there. And there."

Those tiny wet kisses on her back were making her inner thighs quiver and her breasts ache. If Aaron didn't stop it she was going to be too weak to make it out the front door, much less to the opening night of a star-studded Broadway play.

"Umm . . . Aaron? Shouldn't we be going soon?"

He fingered one of the dangly pearl earrings he'd given her that night he'd taught her to shoot pool, how to sniff and sip a glass of fine wine, and introduced her to her biggest weakness besides him—lobster.

"The limo can wait. This can't." He reached into his coat, then swept his hands around her waist. He opened a slender black velvet box and withdrew three rows of pearls attached to a heart-shaped gold clasp that had sparkling red stones set inside it.

"I thought about diamonds, but rubies suit you better. It's more than just your color"—he draped the pearls around her neck and locked the dazzling clasp at her throat—"it's *you*."

Tracing the heart, she sighed. "Aaron, it's too much."

"No such thing," he promptly informed her. He slid his white-gloved fingers between her red-tipped nails. The sight of their hands touching just so, fingertips flirting with the ruby heart and palms laid together over the rise of her bosom, was a picture too sweeping for words.

"What have you done to me?" he said in an intimate whisper. "No one else knows me like you do, no one's made me feel like you do. You've got me under one hell of a spell."

So it would seem, was Addy's thought. Aaron switched moods more often than he changed clothes, but this was one side of him that she'd never encountered before.

"Why'd you give me this necklace?" she asked softly.

"I gave it to you because I wanted to. And because it matches your earrings. But most of all because it's my way of saying thank you."

"It's certainly an extravagant thanks, Aaron. Whatever did I do to deserve such a beautiful thing?"

"Just being you is more than reason enough. But there is another reason. Come on, I'll show it to you." He draped the lace shawl she'd laid out over her shoulders. With his arm around her, his touch conveyed a feeling that was too potent to possibly miss. There was an urgency in him, a hunger that was so awesomely ferocious, it was frightening to imagine it unleashed from his tether of restraint. In fact, when they reached the studio and he murmured, "Close your eyes," Addy wondered if she dared.

Once she did, he turned her around. Then his arm was no longer around her, and she suddenly longed for the feel of that unsettling desire in him that was tremulously dark, definitely dangerous.

She heard the rustle of a sheet dropping to the floor, a sigh of satisfaction come from Aaron. There was an unmistakable note of anticipation in his voice when he said, "Expressions can't lie. Let me see yours now. *Look.*"

Knowing that her opinion mattered so very much to him, she hesitated, fearful that her unmasked reaction might dampen his excitement. Addy swore to herself that she'd love whatever it was on sight.

She opened her eyes.

"*My word,*" she whispered. "Oh my word, Aaron. I don't believe what I'm seeing." What she saw seemed to float out from the wall, *to breathe.* The sculpture had glorious hair flowing over the rise of naked breasts, and a face of passion and innocence, with lips parted as if begging for a kiss. And the hand extending out seemed to beckon her to leap inside the frame that contained the very essence of her.

"How could a simple mountain girl ever be so glorified as this?" she asked in disbelief, moving closer.

"There is no glorification here, Addy. Quite simply, she's you." He bent and kissed the fingertips. It was then that she realized there was a ring on the woman's hand.

Her hand. Unable to take her eyes off the sculpture, Addy fingered the aged gold band she wore. Never had she felt so honored to be wedded to Aaron, a man who would pay such majestic tribute to a woman he'd yet to claim as his.

And never had she felt so dwarfed in his shadow, so unable to make him proud enough to deserve something like this.

He moved behind her and rested his palms on her shoulders. "I'm glad you like it."

"Like it? I can't even describe my feelings. They're as overwhelming as—as you."

His laughter was soft, but what he pressed against her bottom was hard as the outcropping of mountain rock. Tracing the ruby heart, he moved against her in a way that was seductive yet oddly sweet in its gentleness. He was so close, she could feel the full measure of him, the faint pulse that felt like a secret heartbeat.

"Something tells me we'd better get going before I prove just how overwhelming I can be." The lick of his tongue tripped down her neck, and she shivered. "Of course, seduction being very much on my mind, I expect you'll be finding out before the night is through."

FIFTEEN

Aaron noticed there was an almost reverent silence that rippled through the low roar of conversation in the Shubert's posh, expansive lobby. The silence followed in Addy's wake as she wound a path to the "powder room," as she called it. He also noticed that more than a few champagne flutes were lifted her way. *Let them look*, he thought. Let them look and covet what he was claiming for his own. *Tonight*.

Tonight was the night he and Addy would become lovers. More than that, he was going to leave no doubt in Addy's mind that she was his wife and he was her husband. She could keep her friends and the independence that was rightfully hers, but leaving him, *ever*, was no longer an option. They were *not* going to be a repeat from his past, because he wasn't going to let it happen. Only a fool would let go the best thing he could ever have in his entire life, and he was no fool. He was just . . . obsessed. Obsessed with his wife.

As Aaron toasted himself in silence, James blew out a low whistle. "My God, man, the woman is absolutely glorious! Divine, delightful, and did I mention, sexy as hell?"

"James, I'm getting jealous." Lawrence took a sip from his silver flask, then pocketed it with a wistful sigh. "But you're right, of course. There's something about her that's refreshingly unique. Where on earth did you find her, Aaron?"

"Half-moon Hollow, where else?" he replied dryly.

James tapped an elbow to Lawrence's ribs. "Aaron's doing stand-up these days." And then, the light, bantering tone gone, he asked with concern, "How *is* it going these days?"

"Are you asking as a friend who cares or a master dealer who couldn't care less just so I hurry the hell up and deliver a mother lode of work?"

"Both. When you called to invite us along, I got the impression the business you refused to discuss back then had some very private overtones that you deemed better saved for now."

"The magic's back," Aaron confided while scanning the crowd. He saw a swish of red satin and sable hair. He smiled broadly, a smile that proclaimed him smitten with his bride.

"James, dear, do you get the impression that our good man here is living with his muse? And not just any muse. One that's absolutely glorious. Divine, delightful, and, oh yes, sexy as hell."

"Hell is right." James let go a long-suffering sigh and then a weary chuckle. "It's obvious she inspires something primitive in you, Aaron, but I don't believe that extends to a certain discipline of art."

"Does that mean you just resigned?"

"No, it means that I *am* resigned. Go with it, do what you have to, which apparently you're doing anyway. When you're ready, we'll figure something out for a showing, one that might prove to be no less than a *je ne sais quoi* event . . . or a bloody massacre. Either way, we'll hang together—let's just hope it's not a public lynching."

"Quiet, here she comes," said Lawrence.

"Indeed, she does. Walking softly with beauty and grace," said James.

And then Aaron said, "Gentleman, behold the magic."

If anyone asked him what the play was about, or even if it was a halfway decent performance, Aaron knew he'd hail it as "Mesmerizing, unrivaled by anything you can imagine."

Only it was Addy, not the play, that he watched. And what he saw was worth more than the price of every ticket in the audience combined. Addy, gripping his hand while she leaned forward with her eyes wide and breath held. Addy, throwing back her head and laughing until tears streamed down her cheeks. Then more tears, and a fist pressed against her breast. And finally, Addy surging from her seat to applaud with a clap that surely deafened the stars on stage.

She was the first to stand. One by one the rest of the audience followed suit. Only Aaron remained seated, memorizing the picture she made. It was a memory to be cherished with the others he'd stored in his mind, his heart.

As the four of them left, her animated chatter gave him such pleasure that Aaron hated to interrupt her.

"Where to from here? It's your big night on the town, Addy. You choose."

"Well . . ." Addy debated. There was, of course, that dance hall where her friends said they hung out on weekends, but she was sure it wasn't the sort of place where her dress or company would fit in. The only appropriate place she could think of was the club she'd auditioned at last Saturday on a dare from Tony. It was classy, and not just anybody could get in. But she did know the bouncer, Sammy, who kept the undesirables out and removed the guests who became undesirable after they were inside.

Sammy would let her in. Knowing that gave her a much needed sense of importance. For once it would be her doing, not Aaron's, that allowed them entrée to a special piece of the world. And maybe, just maybe . . . She smiled with a sudden idea. Why, after Aaron saw what a fancy club this was . . . And if he was bent on seduction, then she did need to hurry up and pay him off. But best of all, she could make him as proud of her as she was of him.

And she could even do it tonight!

"I've got the perfect spot," she announced, clicking her heels with anticipation. "I hear the food's good but the entertainment's even better."

"Then what are we waiting for? Name the place." She did, and the three men exchanged glances. Aaron raised a brow. "If that's where you really want to go, Addy, I should be able to get us in."

"No need," she told him proudly, waving aside his offer. "*I'll* get us in." At his dubious look she lifted her nose. "You'll see. And, Aaron, don't you dare try to beat me to it."

After the limo pulled up, the driver was beat to Addy's door by a gorilla-sized bouncer who rushed over the second she rolled down her window and called, "Howdy, Sammy!"

"What are you doing here, Addy?" he said with a big grin that had Aaron's smile tightening. And then it disappeared altogether when Sammy gave her a hug and Addy whispered something in his ear. He nodded, and she put a finger to her lips, leaving no doubt that she and Sammy shared a secret.

Sammy motioned the rest of them out, and Addy made a quick round of introductions. First Lawrence and James.

"And this is my—well, this here is . . ."

"Aaron Breedlove," he filled in, unsmiling. And then his lips curved a little at Sammy's slight grimace, as

Aaron gripped his hand. Aaron let go and put his arm around Addy. Tight.

Sammy followed them inside and made sure they got the best seats available. He bent down near Addy's ear, and Aaron strained to listen. All he caught was something about the manager and "no problem."

There was a problem all right. Every instinct Aaron possessed shouted it loud and clear. Something that went beyond Addy's secret life that didn't include him was about to happen. After their orders were quickly taken, the conversation seemed to revolve around the play. Aaron managed to contribute only a few monosyllable answers and an occasional nod.

And then Sammy was nodding at Addy. The pianist was nodding at Addy. And then Aaron knew.

He could only shake his head.

"Be right back," she chirped. She pecked him on the cheek, and there she went. Addy on her way.

"What *is* the matter?" James asked, concerned.

"She's going to sing," he said without inflection.

"But what's wrong with that? Good God, Aaron, you look as if you just lost your dearest friend for life."

"That about sums it up." The drinks arrived, and he had his double Crown Royal tossed down before the waitress left. "Another." He tapped the glass while he watched Addy tap her foot beside the grand piano spilling out a bluesy intro.

She lifted the microphone to her lips, intimate as a kiss. She hadn't sung more than two soaring stanzas when every ripple of conversation in the room ceased.

Her eyes were on him, and it was as if she were singing to him alone. Breaking his gaze away, he looked around and realized he wasn't the only one completely dazzled. Everyone was riveted to her, and fear began to fill his heart. He would lose her. He'd never been more convinced of that fact.

The song seemed to last forever. Each aching note from her lips felt like a knife plunged into his heart. The last one she sustained nearly finished him off then and there.

What little was left of his hope, his determination to secure their future together, was put to a quick but painful death. In silence he stood as the audience rose to their feet, as if by some magical mass accord. And as if in slow motion, he saw their wrists bend, their palms meet, hands reaching to the center of tables to slowly lift the fresh flowers that rained like teardrops at her feet.

He wanted to weep.

He distantly felt James's grip on his shoulder, distantly heard him shout over the roar, "I thought you said that she was going to sing. That wasn't singing, it was—good Lord what was it? A choir of angels, a . . . a—"

"A dream," he said dully. Aaron tossed down the drink set in front of him faster than the first. "A rainbow beyond reach." Not bothering to count them he slapped down several bills and got up. "I'm sorry, but I've got to go. The three of you take the limo. I'll catch a cab home."

SIXTEEN

The space between the table and the sidewalk seemed an endless distance, as endless as the chasm that had opened between where he'd sat and Addy stood on the flower-strewn stage.

Ignoring the limo and the taxis waiting outside, Aaron began to walk. Hands shoved into his pockets, his gaze on the concrete, he heard the rapid click of high heels.

"Aaron! Aaron, wait!"

He kept walking. When she caught up, Addy spun him around. Confusion and hurt filled her eyes, covering the flush of excitement still on her face.

"Where are you going?" she panted. "Why did you leave?"

"I, ah—I'm sorry that I spoiled your moment of glory—it was a real jerk thing for me to do. But the truth is, I left because you'll be leaving me and I couldn't handle it."

"That's the most ridiculous thing I ever heard in my life! For heaven's sake, Aaron, I was only trying to make you proud of me."

"That you did, Addy. You made me very proud. But I'm always proud of you, remember that."

"*Remember?* You make it sound like I'm already gone."

"Not yet, but you'll go. Soon." He hitched a thumb in the club's direction. "You can't walk away from that."

"But I did, except I ran more than I walked." She took his arm. "Seems that we need to talk. Let's walk until we're all talked out. Then we'll catch a taxi home."

For a good while they strolled in silence. He cherished that, Addy's way of always knowing what he needed and supplying it without a moment's thought.

"Wait," she said. He watched her go to a dark huddle that he hadn't even seen. It was a bum, brown paper bag between his knees, shivering from what Aaron suspected was an empty bottle and an unmet need for more. But as usual, Addy saw differently. She took off her shawl, the only covering she had, and laid it over him. "God bless you," Aaron heard her whisper before she returned and explained, "He was cold."

A random act of kindness and beauty, that's what it was, and that part of Addy's nature he truly believed would never change.

He shrugged off his coat and pulled it around her shoulders, knowing his own act was anything but random. Quite simply, he wanted to cover her with anything, everything that was a part of him. Given that, he was being more selfish than kind.

The minutes ticked by as Aaron gathered his thoughts. Finally, he said, "When I was about your age and had a year under my belt on the outside, I met a woman who was quite a bit older than me. Her name was Lisa." Remembering her as he'd seen her then, he smiled wistfully. "She was lovely. Lovely to look at, to listen to, I could even watch the way she moved for hours."

"Then you were in love with her." An unmistakable distress in Addy's quiet voice caused him to pull her closer.

"Oh, I thought I was. Very much at the time. She was everything I wanted to be—cultured, confident, worldly. I suppose coming from a wealthy background had something to do with that. Lisa had good breeding. But she was also bored. Bored of charity functions, bored of shopping, bored of her yearly trips to Europe. Bored of her rich old husband." He paused, letting that sink in. "You can imagine how flattered I was when she took a personal interest in me. I couldn't fathom why she did at the time, but in retrospect I believe that I amused her. My art, however, she did take seriously."

"How . . . how did you meet?"

"Outside of a store." He shot Addy a sideways glance. "She was going in while I was coming out of a small art gallery with an armful of my paintings the dealer hadn't wanted any more than he wanted me in there. I have to admit, the work was pretty rough; me, I was even rougher. My clothes, my speech, my manners—they all left a lot to be desired.

"Anyway, Lisa thought my work had great potential. She had money to burn and offered to support me and introduce me to the right people—after she polished up the outside package. I guess you could say that I was like a pet project of sorts. She had a good time grooming me, and I soaked it up, so eager to please that it was laughable. Her approval was very important to me. Can you guess where I'm going with this?"

"I think so. You became her lover, didn't you?"

"Considering all the time we spent together, I guess it's no surprise. She had everything I thought I wanted, and for a while I was blinded by all of the money, the glamour, the power."

Addy stopped walking. In her eyes was a wealth of understanding. She knew this was hard for him, that it was hurting his pride. "You don't have to tell me any more."

"Yes, Addy, I do. It's as important for you to hear this as it is for me to get it out of my system." Urging her on at an unhurried pace, he continued telling his story. "After a couple of years things changed—the balance of power tipped the other way. Thanks to Lisa's contacts, my career was off the ground and starting to soar. I was grateful to her, of course—and I still am—but by my second showing, the raves were rolling in. And with them came certain perks, besides the money."

"You mean, like learning to fly and having your own plane?"

"That was a nice side benefit, and one that Lisa didn't mind. What she had a problem with was finding me in bed with one of the women who made themselves available to me. There were quite a few she didn't know about, or maybe she just looked the other way, knowing

I was young and feeling my oats. Anyway, it was quite a scene. She was throwing everything that she'd done for me in my face, crying because I'd told her that I loved her and she had believed me, and then begging me to put it all behind us so we could start over. Things went downhill from there."

"But, Aaron, how could it get any worse than that?"

"Like I told you before, desperate people are dangerous people. She was desperate. She threatened, she pleaded. She left her husband."

"Oh, no."

At Addy's soft groan he assured her, "Oh, yes. It got worse than horrible. I started feeling suffocated and desperate myself to be free of her. I'm afraid that I ended up treating her badly. I moved out of my apartment and didn't leave a forwarding address. I cut my ties with the dealer she'd convinced to take a chance on me and hooked up with James. So, everyone knew I'd ended it—a public humiliation on top of the personal turmoil. Lisa couldn't handle it. She tracked me down and started following me." He shuddered, remembering. "The whole thing was totally out of control."

"Aaron, that had to be frightening for you. What happened?" Addy asked, anxiously. "What'd you do?"

"You're right, it did get scary. After ignoring her, warning her, and doing my best to hide from her didn't work, I went to the police. I hated to do it, but I didn't see any other option. I had her slapped with a restraining order. After that, I guess you could say that Lisa bottomed out. What friends she had left were very concerned, and they tried to convince me to go see her.

In a private mental hospital. I felt responsible for her breakdown, but I couldn't bring myself to do it.

"No, Aaron," Addy urgently assured him. "It wasn't your doing; it was her own. It was her decision to be your benefactor, her decision to step out on her husband, and her decision to throw everything away for nothing. Folks have to take responsibility for their own actions; they have no right to lay blame on someone else. Don't go blaming yourself."

"I don't—at least not anymore." He looked at her then, his gaze relaying the import of what he was about to say. "But I can't blame her either. You see, Addy, sometimes, where certain people are involved, emotions can take over and rob an otherwise good person of both pride and reason. It could happen to anyone. Even me."

Addy slowly shook her head, refusing to believe. He simply nodded, once, and whispered firmly, "Yes."

A silence fell between them. Several minutes passed before Addy broke it. "Did you ever see her again?"

"About three years ago, I saw her in a restaurant and pretended not to see her. She was with her husband. Lisa appeared frail, not at all the woman I first met— all that shimmering loveliness gone. There was a vacant look about her—like the house was there, but nobody was home. Her husband looked happy, though, pleased in a perverse sort of way. I thought the sight was chilling, and yet—yet . . ."

"What?"

"A part of me understood how he must feel. Wanting and loving someone he couldn't really have, probably needing her in every way possible while she only needed him for practical purposes. And then, to finally have her where he wanted her—dependent, leaning on the strength of his weakness for her. I pitied them."

"Yes," Addy agreed, "it is sad."

"What seemed saddest to me was the fact that a lot of pain could have been avoided." He snorted in disgust. "I'm not excusing what I did, or Lisa's role in it either. But I'll tell you what, if I'd been her husband, I never would have stood by while my wife carried on an affair under my nose. She was looking for some excitement in her life, and believe me, if I'd been he, I would have given her some all right. He should have put down his foot, and I mean *hard*. And if that hadn't worked, he should have fought for her. Lisa would have respected that."

"What woman wouldn't?" was Addy's reply. And then she asked him, "Would you fight to keep me? Tell me the truth, Aaron."

The truth was, if he saw Addy in bed with another man, he'd surely end up doing hard time behind bars. He wouldn't think beyond the instinct to kill the bastard.

"If you were my wife, any fighting to be had would be between you and me, no one else. If someone touches my wife, we're talking a death wish. As for you, if I even suspected you were cheating on me . . . I'm not really sure what I'd do. I'd never hit you, but there are other ways to punish someone. I have the capacity to be cruel, I learned that from Lisa. I'm afraid I'd use any means I had to make you pay in spades."

"But, Aaron, I would never cheat on you."

He gave a curt nod. "I reckon that's so. You have too much moral fiber to ever do such a thing. Besides,

I'd keep you too exhausted emotionally and physically to leave so much as . . . a scrap of leftovers for anyone else."

She chuckled softly at that, her easy humor falling over him like a waterfall mist. But then she grew serious and said firmly, "Seems to me that you're forgetting something, Aaron. I am your wife."

Feeling as if he'd laid himself bare only for Addy to flail him raw, he turned on her.

"You don't get it, do you?" he snapped. "Wise up, Addy! That can't happen now. It's too late, okay? Things are going to change, *fast*. What we had, could have had, is on its way out. Gone, over. Out with the old, in with the new. New friends, new pressures and obligations, a new career that'll squeeze everything it can out of you and leave precious little for anything else. You're on your way, babe. Up and over the top. God, didn't you see the way those people were looking at you? Look at *me* and tell me that you didn't love it so much that you can't wait to experience it again. Tell me that you hadn't been offered a job at that club before we got there tonight."

"Well, yes, but—but, I didn't take it."

"You will. You have to. It's between us now. Maybes and might-have-beens have a way of souring a relationship once the honeymoon's over and reality sets in. This is the reality of it, Addy. I was foolish enough, selfish enough, to believe we finally had enough to make a marriage work. It was a simple equation: I love you, you love me, equals happily ever after."

"You mean that—that you love me?"

"Of course I do! *Damn you*. Damn you for making me love you the way that I do. I'm so blind with it, I conveniently forgot to figure in the inevitable. You have a rare gift—"

"But so do you!"

"Apples and oranges, pudding and pie. I thrive on solitude, you thrive on people. You gravitate to people, and they gravitate to you. They'll be coming at you from every direction, especially men, lots of men. Call it self-discovery, call it curiosity, I don't care what the hell you call it, but you'll have to satisfy it sooner or later."

An image of her satisfying him, bathing him with her tongue, drying that coveted moisture with her hair, had him tightening up. His hands, his gut, his heart, became tight fists squeezing every drop of life he had into the part of him that extended, distended, in its fruitless search, an endless need to burrow himself in a haven called home. Addy was home. Not Half-moon Hollow, not New York, not even a loft that would be no more than a still-life study in emptiness without the life she breathed into it.

"The only reason I haven't satisfied it, Aaron, is because you keep pulling away before I can get more than a taste." She leveled him with an accusing, determined gaze. And then she proceeded to devastate the tenuous grip he held on his consuming need to savor her, to devour her body and spirit. Addy threw off his coat. She reached for the zipper hidden in the side of her designer gown.

Self-preservation took hold. He gripped her hand.

"Let go," she hissed. "I want my taste, Aaron. And if miracles still happen, just maybe you'll realize that the only reason you don't trust me to stay true to you is because you lack trust in people, including yourself. Let's do it. *Now*."

She gripped the front of his shirt and did her best to drag him to the dark alley just behind them. She jerked and jerked, but he was unmovable.

In a steely voice he ground out, "I am not about to 'do it' with you in an alley." Thunder rumbled in the distance. "Rain's on the way. Put my coat back on. We're catching the first cab that passes."

She lifted her face to the darkening sky. "I love the thunder. I love the rain. I love *you*. Yesterday, today, tomorrow. Believe it, Aaron. Believe it and make love to me. In a dark alley, in the elevator, on a fancy bed or on a dirt floor, *I don't care*. Just make love to me and believe in me the way that I believe in you."

She believed in him, his heart sang. Even after all the reasons he'd given her not to, she believed in him. If only.

If only he could somehow believe that the temptations sure to come her way wouldn't strip her from his needful, desperate arms. If only . . .

If only he weren't so desperate to take what he could while he still had the chance, he could save all the goodness they had gathered between them instead of feeding it like fuel to a destructive, unquenchable flame.

"Only a fool believes in waking up to a dream, Addy. And only a fool would wake himself up before a sweet dream was over just so he could stare a brutal reality in the face." As if heaven had decided he deserved some small bit of mercy, a cab came out of nowhere and slowed at the wave of his hand. "Get in," he said, his tone short as his tether.

"Where are we going?"

"To 'do it' in more familiar surroundings." The door shut, the address delivered, he pulled her from where she sat arm to arm, thigh to thigh, onto his lap.

"My bed or yours?" she whispered in his ear.

"Neither."

"But you mean to take me all the same—as your wife?"

He gripped her hips, pulling them down against his own. "Wives and husbands, they're together forever if it's right. For us that remains a question that only time can answer. For tonight we're lovers. For now I don't want to think about tomorrow."

"Then what do you want to think about?"

Shutting his mind to the self-recriminations sure to come, he softly bit her bottom lip as he slid his palm up her dress. Squeezing her bottom possessively, he murmured, "I don't want to think about anything except you and me."

"Because you love me." She licked at his chin, then pulled back, giving him a smile beyond sublime.

"Oh, yes," he assured her. "Madly, insanely, I'm consumed with it." He tightened his intimate grip. "In fact, I love you so much that I want to give you one last chance to change your mind."

"I don't want it. I'll take my chances with you."

"Then you'd better kiss the dice for luck." He kissed her thoroughly. "I thought you were listening, but just in case you didn't hear me, you'd better get this: Lovers,

Addy, don't need rings or vows to start making demands. The more desperate they are, the more demanding they get."

"And are you . . . desperate?"

He laughed harshly. "Desperate and more. You're digging yourself in deeper, babe. Lie down with me, and you'll never be free of me again."

How much it had cost him to give her one last out.

"We're here," she said, getting out of the cab. "Let's get ourselves inside so you can start making your demands."

It seemed to him that her ignorance was, for now, bliss for them both. She was oblivious to the roll of thunder as they entered the apartment building. Addy loved the thunder; she loved the rain. And he loved her beyond pride or reason. All he could do was pray that by God's mercy they might some way, somehow, weather the storm ahead.

Together.

SEVENTEEN

By the time he unlocked the door, Aaron's shirt was off, and her bodice was hugging her waist.

"I love you," she vowed with more certainty than the vows she had taken beneath a half-moon.

"Don't say it." His teeth nipped at her lips in a loving but stern chastisement. "Promise me you won't say that again. Not until you know that it's me, and only me, you could ever want."

"I want you now."

"And for now, that has to be enough for us both."

"Make it enough," she begged—she demanded—kicking the door shut and hastily flipping the dead-bolt lock.

"I can't." He tossed off her shoes, peeled off panties and hose. He licked the inside of her knee while his hands wedged apart her unsteady legs. Parting her even more intimately, he wore an expression of pure pleasure and dark longing. And then he blew a whisper against her. "With us, Addy, there's no such thing as enough."

"Try," she beseeched him.

"Consider it your dying wish."

He made her die a thousand deaths and more with his fingers, his tongue, his words, before she slumped to the floor.

Her eyes closed in ecstasy, she heard the sounds of him rapidly getting rid of his clothes. "Look at me."

She did, and gloried in the naked need in his eyes, his face. The expanse of his chest was covered with pale hair that grew darker as it descended. The evidence of his gender extended proud and mighty. From there her gaze roamed over two spread legs, strong as David's, large as Goliath's.

It seemed the most natural thing she should do to press kisses to both his feet, then sweep her hair across them.

"Oh God," she heard him moan high above her. And then his hands were on her, lifting her up and into his arms. Time had no meaning, and suddenly, they were there, in the studio, and Aaron was saying, "I want to make love here. Then every time I work, I'll remember this. Please, Addy, please. No matter what, never forget this. Never forget me."

How strange it seemed that he should even ask. How could she possibly forget the sight of him putting her down to fluff up a clean stack of drop cloths so that they resembled a pile of pure white hay. How could she possibly forget him gently laying her down upon it, straddling her thighs, then holding up a delicate paintbrush as if it were a conquering sword.

From her face to her throat to her cleft he stroked her with the assurance, the sensitivity, of a master artist in a passionate frenzy.

The response he claimed from her was wondrous, hot and sweet. There was no pride to be had in begging for release from this mindless, writhing, delicious misery. Laying the brush aside, he closed his mouth over her breast, suckling her until her hips rose, and her legs parted wide.

"More. Please, *more*."

"How much more?" he taunted, probing her ever so gently.

"Everything you have. All of you." Her body cried out for him, only to grasp . . . nothing. "Give me," she demanded. Desperation rising, she gripped him and tried to force him inside. "*Give me*," she said again.

And then he was in her, thrusting with shallow strokes that made her twist beneath him in a luxurious discomfort while her hips rose in search of the ultimate pleasure.

Of pain.

She shrieked. He cried out her name with an equal agony.

For a while he did not move. His eyes searching hers, he whispered, "I'm sorry, so sorry. I never want to hurt you." He began to withdraw. She dug her fingers into his buttocks and locked her thighs tightly over his.

"You're too tight," he told her, as if she didn't know.

"Stay where you are," she gasped out. "And don't you dare try to leave me until this is finished."

His arms braced above her shoulders, his head fell forward, and a trickle of sweat fell upon the single tear she couldn't hold back.

He murmured softly to her as he stroked her cleft, helping her body to adjust to his.

She winced slightly as she moved beneath him. "The time has come, Aaron, when blood is better shared than shed."

He pulled up, and at her cry of protest he plunged deep.

Thunder. Lightning. Without and within, the storm gathered strength with a fury. Their coupling was ferocious and too needy and poignant for words. Wordlessly, he urged her over, and willingly she went down on hands and knees.

His teeth raking over her nape, she heard him command, "*Come*. Please, come. For me, Addy. *Only for me*."

Only for him would she ever bow to such an uncompromising demand. For an untellable space of time her mind was rendered as helpless as her body, controlled by the jerks from his hips. Rapture. It was rapture she embraced within this ultimate surrender. No sense of herself. No sense of him. Only a sense of them, a man and a woman with no beginning, no end.

He was thrusting into her in a frenzy of possession.

Then, suddenly, he pulled away from her, and her back was wet. As he collapsed on top of her, she wondered why he hadn't found his release within her, and then felt a rush of love and gratitude at his concern and protection of her.

His left hand gripped hers. Their rings met.

His lips in her hair, he panted, "Are you all right?"

His weight heavy, she wheezed out, "Never better."
I love you.

His soft chuckle caressed her back. Then he was beside her, stroking her cheek, his eyes telling her that he loved her more than life itself.

She was so caught up in the soundless message of his gaze that she was caught by surprise when he whispered, "Open your legs."

Even more surprising was the tickle of the brush, soothing the tender flesh he had breached. He stared at her with a look akin to reverence—until he took away the brush and got up.

He went to the goddesslike sculpture she still couldn't believe was her. He lifted the brush, and traced the snowy-white lips, then filled them in.

Turning, he said with a tender smile, "Such is the difference between an enviable rough draft and a masterpiece."

Addy opened her arms. Aaron kissed the brush, then threw it aside. He claimed her offering, and she held him close.

"Such a master you are," she said, her sigh content.

"And you, Addy, you are my master"—he kissed her softly—"because when you're not giving me hell, you give me such peace."

For three days they did not leave the loft. Addy thought their time together a rare and precious thing, a time of priceless passion, discovery, trust given and treated with care. It was a time outside of time and place. And it was theirs, only theirs. With the phone unhooked, the only sounds of life outside their own were those that rose from the bustling street beneath them.

On the fourth day Aaron woke her with a kiss and breakfast in bed. But there was something amiss.

"You've got on your clothes. How come?"

His smile seemed oddly strained. "Life goes on, Addy. We can't stay naked forever, unfortunately. And, unfortunately, we need to talk."

She knew he meant a different kind of talking than whispered secrets shared on a pillow or beneath the sheets.

"I don't want to talk about this, Aaron."

"But we have to. Pretending it's not there won't make it go away." When she waved aside the breakfast tray, he put it down and began to pace, a sure sign their special time and place was coming to an end. "You'll take the job, of course. The sooner you start, the better, before I start trying to change your mind. Despite telling myself I wouldn't try to do that, I know that I might."

In disbelief she asked him, "After all that we've shared, surely you're not still afraid of me leaving you?"

His glance was sharp. "After all that we've shared, I'm more afraid of that than ever. Even more afraid of what I might do if it happens. But that's not the only reason why I'd try to keep you here all to myself."

He faced her squarely. "The emotional stakes are high. But professionally, they are too." He tapped his temple. "Up here, I know that any career you have is just as important as mine. But what's up there doesn't always carry through in my actions. My intentions are good, but my behavior doesn't necessarily follow, you know?"

"What I know is that I'm not about to let you down when you need me the most. I'll still be your model, Aaron. I want to be."

He blew out a sigh of relief. "You don't know how good that is to hear. Because without you there can be no showing, and that could polish off what little's left of my own career. But that still leaves us with a problem. If you're working nights, pulling a day job is going to be awfully tough. I don't have to tell you how demanding I can be or how tired you can get after posing for hours on end."

It was true. Even so, she hastened to assure him, "Don't worry about me, I'll manage just fine."

"You can be spread only so thin, Addy. If you're burning a candle at both ends, eventually you'll burn out. I don't want that to happen to you." He held up his hands. "If you've got any suggestions on how to work this out, I'd sure like to hear them."

She thought about it for a bit. Aaron was right; she did have to sleep sometime. The club's manager had offered her a princely sum to sing, but he'd told her the only nights he could give her off would be Sunday and Monday. The rest of the week she'd need to be there by five to practice with Mort, the piano player, and the last set wouldn't be finished until midnight. And it was a long ride, both ways. All in all, Aaron was going to get shorted, especially if she took off on her Saturdays that she so greatly prized.

It was a hard decision, but one she didn't think twice about making. "Except for Mondays, Aaron, I'm sorry to say that I'll have to cut back on my weekly hours with you. But I'll make them up on Saturdays and Sundays. How's that?"

A smile lit his face. Then slowly dissolved. "The Sundays I'll take. But your Saturdays are too important to you. It wouldn't be right for me to rob you of them."

Addy got up and wrapped her arms around him.

"To rob someone, Aaron, you have to take something away that they're not willing to give." Lifting her face to his, she offered everything that was in her. "I give you my Saturdays, and I give them to you gladly."

"You're an amazing woman, Addy." His palms cupping her behind, he pulled her against him. "So amazing, in fact, that even if it's a miracle either of us can still walk, I'm ready to make tracks to the kitchen."

"The kitchen?" she asked, laughing as he hauled her over his shoulder and took a playful bite of her rump. "But you already made me breakfast."

"*Making* you for breakfast is what I've got in mind. Let's see, I think I'll have you sunny-side up—after I get out the butter."

"Ummm . . . just thinking about it's making me hungry too. So, what do I get to eat?"

Aaron laughed seductively. "There's plenty of sausage."

EIGHTEEN

Addy dabbed on some extra concealer beneath her eyes. She decided that she looked as if she'd aged two years in the two months since she'd taken on two jobs. Of course, she might have been able to muster the energy to keep up if she didn't have a man in bed who was as demanding a lover as he was an employer. Lord, when *was* she supposed to sleep!

She'd had her chance the night before, since Aaron had worked till dawn, but her conscience had kept her awake until he joined her. After a kiss good morning, he was sawing logs while she still fretted over whether she'd taken on more than she could handle.

Aaron's prophecy that men would come at her with every kind of invitation imaginable had proved true. She had turned down each one. All of them except for Bruce.

She had liked him on sight, when he introduced himself as a friend of Tony's, then swept down in a most gallant bow. Tony had sent a message that he and the gang really missed her, but they were thrilled about her overnight success.

Thinking about it, Addy's guilt doubled. At last a Saturday afternoon free, and she wasn't spending it with her dear friends who no doubt believed she'd rather bask in her good fortune than be with them. But worst of all was Aaron so gladly allowing her this time to herself when she meant to commit no small betrayal.

Addy closed her eyes in exhaustion and distress.

She felt his palms rest on her shoulders. And then she felt the rough texture of his cheek pressing against hers. Steeling herself, she opened her eyes and saw their faces paired in the mirror. His expression was loving, longing.

"I don't suppose you're up for a quickie." He winked.

"I reckon you suppose right." She forced a smile.

"Well, it's your time off anyway," he said casually, but she was aware of a slight tensing in his hold. "And besides, there's always tonight."

Sometimes she thought they were too tuned in to each other. This was one of those times. Aaron knew something was up; she was sure of it. Stifling a groan, she prayed for a new talent: the ability to tell a convincing lie.

"It's not that I don't want to spend my time with you. It's just that I—I need to work with Mort on some new songs, so we're getting together for lunch before we practice."

"Got a date with Mort, huh?"

"Don't worry, we'll be chaperoned by his piano." Addy managed a light laugh.

"Tell you what, if you really do want to spend your well-deserved free time with me, why don't I throw on something presentable and join you and Mort. It's been a while since I elbowed my way in. Think you could use your clout and get me the best seat? I'll be your groupie for the night," he teased.

"No! I mean—I mean there's some special folks who're supposed to show up, and I promised that I'd sit at their table between sets. I'd rather you come tomorrow night instead."

Aaron's face clouded. "I see," he said, watching her much too closely in the mirror. "Far be it from me to intrude when you have important people to visit with."

"But you're important too, and—"

"Look, you don't have to baby-sit my ego," he said sharply. He paused, then said in a much nicer tone, "Sorry, Addy. I'm a big boy, and you're a big girl with a big career in the making. You've done wonders to get mine on a new track, and I'm not about to repay you by heaping on more stress than what you've already got. I want you to succeed. When life's good for you, babe, it's good for me."

The last he said so sincerely, she couldn't doubt it. But did he have to go nuzzling her neck the way he did when he wanted to make her melt? Darn Aaron anyway! It was just like him to be extra sweet and make her feel worse than ever.

He picked up the silver antique brush he'd given her on opening night and pulled it through her hair. "A hundred strokes now," he murmured, "and a thousand when you get home."

"Think we could settle on half the strokes and twice as many hugs?"

The brush stilled. "You can have as many hugs as you want, when you want. As for those strokes, I'd rather not give you any than so much as one that you didn't want."

"Why, Aaron, surely you realize that I love our love-making," she hastened to assure him. "But the truth is, I'm tuckered out lately and, well, keeping up with you takes a lot of energy. You're a wonderful lover, but you're also a very lusty man."

Addy was relieved to see his slow smile. Seldom did he show any insecurity about their relationship, intimate or otherwise. But it was there, slipping out in tattletale moments such as this, and when it happened, she noticed he rubbed his ring like a genie's magic lamp.

"You do look tired to me," he said, scrutinizing her reflection while he worked his ring. "Why don't you plan to take a few days off from posing? I can work around you."

"Absolutely not. You've got that showing lined up with James for next month, and you can't spare me a few days off. Besides, I can always catnap if I'm posing lying down." More than once she'd awakened to the smell of dinner cooking and a sheet tucked around her that hadn't been there when she'd nodded off.

"We'll talk about it later," he informed her.

Addy shook a finger at him. "I'm on to you and your wily ways, Aaron Breedlove. What you mean is, *you'll* talk me into whatever it is you've already decided. For all your big-city airs, deep down you're made of other stuff."

"What kind of stuff?" he asked testily.

"If you ask me nicely, I just might tell you."

"Please?" A yank of the brush.

A fight was brewing. And though she knew she ought to back off and baby-sit that ego of his, her tongue got loose before she could catch it.

"Let's just say that you're a lot more like your papa than you think. It's either your way or no way, oh great chosen son who likes to rule the roost. When you want to eat, we eat. When you say it's time to work, we work. Time to go shopping? Off we go—unless you're of a mind to change your mind and want to get naked instead. The fact is, you like to be king around the house and—"

"Hold it! You just hold it right there." He started brushing her hair with hard, stinging strokes. "I am an enlightened, *civilized* man, and you are lucky to have me. I take good care of you and ask for precious little in return. You're gone at night when I want you home with me, but do I say anything? Hell, no! I keep my mouth shut while you go on and on about your exciting new life that doesn't include me. A lesser man might be jealous, but not me, no sir. I've given you your space and all the time you need to decide if you want a lifetime commitment instead of this shack-up arrangement that doesn't suit me one damn bit."

She chewed on her tongue to keep from reminding Aaron that it had been *his* idea. As for him giving her plenty of space, hogwash! She'd had more of that when she'd lived in a bedroom the size of a slop jar with Loretta. And time? Hah! He was simply biding his while she spread hers too thin. Aaron was only kidding himself if he thought he had her fooled, but airing that load of dirty laundry was best saved for later. She had an appointment with Bruce, and if she tore into Aaron, they'd be tangling for hours.

"Lip service," she muttered, and smacked away his brush-wielding hand.

"Excuse me?" Aaron sent the brush sailing onto the bed. "Do you care to repeat that?"

"Not worth repeating." Addy glanced at her watch, a fake-jeweled bit of fun she'd bought with her own money. She couldn't miss Aaron's thunderous scowl. He'd given her a diamond-and-ruby timepiece, and though he hadn't said so, she knew it vexed him that she preferred to wear her flashy, cheap one instead. Adding silent fuel to the fire, she searched her jewelry box and passed over his Cartier necklace and earrings for some costume jewelry she'd also bought with her earnings.

All Aaron's prattling on about her independence and them being equals was a load of manure, and she had the savings to prove it. Why, he refused to let her pay for so much as a shared meal!

She whipped on a light cape, grabbed her purse, and headed to the front door, Aaron close on her heels.

"Where do you think you're going?" he demanded, removing her fingers from the lock. "We're not through with this yet."

"Yes, I do believe you're right." She dug out several large bills and stuffed them into Aaron's pants pocket. "I'm buying the groceries this week, and don't you dare put up a fuss the way you did in the store the last time we went shopping and I tried to pay. *I pay my way*. And for once, would you quit trying to buy me!"

His face darkened as he crammed the money back into her palm. Addy dropped the crumbled bills on the floor. She was proud of what she'd earned, dammit, and this time she wasn't about to let Aaron rob her of the right to her self-sufficient pride.

"I don't want your spare change," he said bullishly, and kicked away the money she was so proud of having earned.

"No more than I want yours," she shot back. "You've fed me and dressed me and kept a roof over my head when I didn't have enough spare change of my own for a fleabag motel. What I had, you gave me. Well, sir, I've got my own money now to save or spend however I please. And how I want to spend it is by paying you back for taking me in. When we're even, then we can talk about the real reason for this argument. Understand?"

His jaw worked back and forth, and then it clenched. So did his empty fist.

"I'll tell you what I understand. You're diminishing what I gladly gave. Rub my nose in it, why don't you? Go ahead, wave one of your paychecks under my nose and tell me it's for back rent."

She'd intended to do just that, but in a much nicer way than digging into her purse and slapping a hefty uncashed paycheck in his face.

"This should take care of the rent this month," she snapped. "If it's short, I'll withdraw more."

Glaring at her offering as if it were dirty, he bit out, "The loft's paid for in full. Put it to better use and buy yourself some new clothes and a tacky watch to match."

Tacky! The last dregs of her exhaustion parted like the Red Sea to a rush of red-hot rage.

"Then consider it my reimbursement for all the clothes you've bought me. And a down payment for all those pearls and rubies and diamonds that feel like chains, locking me into a dungeon basement. Next thing I know, you'll be wanting to use them instead of silk scarves to tie me to the bed! But after this, don't you so much as try. I'd rather be put on the rack than be a prisoner in your bed."

In a flash he had her against the door with his hand up her black leather skirt and under her fishnet hose. His cupping palm and adroit fingers had her fighting him in earnest before she was reduced to a pool of ecstasy in his manipulative, possessive hand.

"If you're a prisoner, it's to desire, babe. Give me a minute, and I'll prove it."

She knew Aaron to be a magnificent lover, but what he did best was shower her with lazy caresses and intimate whispers after they were sated and lying in each other's arms. If he got his way with her now, he'd have her right where he wanted her once he was done, all nice and cozy while he talked her into making up.

She didn't want to make up, not now at least. Desperate to get loose, she reached for his crotch. But rather than fondle him, she squeezed until he removed his own grip with a nasty curse. With shaking hands she pushed down her skirt. She left her money and check on the floor, turning from Aaron as he stuffed them into her purse. She worked fast on the remaining locks and headed for the elevator.

Not a lock in Half-moon Hollow. Lord but she was homesick. The urge was strong to stand up Bruce and let the club get a new singer. And if Aaron wanted her? Let him hunt her down and fight to win back her affection.

He slung her purse out so hard, the glittery silver mesh struck the elevator doors.

"Go on and go, but you remember this: You can't buy back what I already claim as mine. And as for reimbursing me for the clothes, consider it done several times over in exchange for modeling fees. Does that make us even? Huh? Think about it *hard*. Real hard. Because once you get home, we're getting this settled once and for all!"

"Don't wait up for me," she informed him, stepping into the elevator, "I'm not sure when I'll be back." She took with her the sweet revenge of Aaron's fist pounding at the crisscrossed iron she shut in his face. As the car descended, she called up, "And don't you even try showing up at the club tonight. Show up and I'll make sure that Sammy throws you out!"

She hit the sidewalk running and had a taxi in seconds. Looking out the back window, she saw Aaron waving furiously to several more cabs that passed him at top speed.

Addy drew in a shuddering breath once she was certain even the fastest cabbie in New York with a hundred-dollar incentive couldn't catch up.

By the time she reached her destination, Addy felt more spiteful than guilty. She gave an extra big tip to the driver with the money that Aaron had refused, then hightailed it through the mirrored double doors and into Bruce's arms.

"Addy! *Darling*. Another minute and I would have called to make sure you hadn't backed out."

"Thank heavens you didn't." Addy gave him a fierce hug while Bruce began to play with her hair. "Got enough fighting on the home front without waging an all-out war. Aaron's going to have a conniption when he finds out where I've been. Fact is, he'd have a hissy fit if he saw you so much as touching me like this."

"Jealous, is he?"

"Way too much. Can't hardly draw a breath without him sucking it up and calling it his own."

"Oh dear, lovers' spat. No?"

"More like a major world war and not a survivor in sight. But that's between Aaron and me, and I don't want you caught in the middle." She dug out the cash she couldn't seem to give away and dropped it in Bruce's wandering hands. "Do us both a favor and take a vacation. My treat, your hide. I'm afraid that Aaron's gonna come hunt you down."

Bruce tucked the wad of bills into her bustier, then snipped at the air with his clippers and laughed. "I'm prepared with my weapon of choice."

"Lord, honey, but I do believe that you could hold your own with a bottle of white lightnin' and pare down a forest with scissors in hand."

Aaron paced like a caged animal while he eyed the phone. He'd called an hour after Addy should have arrived at the club even in standstill traffic, but no answer.

The second time he called, Mort had answered. No, there had been no lunch or practice, but Addy should be there any minute. Call three, Addy was running late. By call four, the crowd was packing in, and the manager was getting worried.

He was worried? What about *him*? Aaron, her lover, and she'd better believe it, her *husband*?

Worry was gnawing at his insides while he was half out of his mind with questions. Why had she lied to him? Where had she gone? Why hadn't she wanted him to be there tonight?

Who was she with? Tony? After all, it was Saturday.

Aaron paced, the phone never out of his sight. Five minutes turned into fifteen, and he grabbed the phone, dialing the club again.

"Is she there yet?" he barked into the receiver. But then he heard her soaring voice in the background and rushed on to say, "Never mind. This is Aaron Breedlove. Reserve a table for me, okay?"

"Sorry, but Ms. McDonald said that you're not to be let in under any circumstances, and she's asked for an escort when she leaves. The boss likes to keep her happy, you understand."

Aaron softly replaced the receiver. How long he stared at the phone, he didn't know. He finally yanked it up and hurled the thing so hard that it shattered against the wall. The smash and the crack of plastic made a satisfying sound. And what kinship he felt with the mangled guts of intricate circuits and wires now exposed.

Aaron worked the gold band on his finger with a fury, all the while wondering if Addy had taken hers off before she went . . . where? It had to be a clandestine meeting. *God, no.* But if not, why had she concocted a nonexistent practice session with Mort?

Aaron's imagination was like a runaway train, barreling headlong without brakes. The questions came at him, and damn, would they never stop? And why did he have to keep remembering that she hadn't wanted him there, even before their fight over the money? The money, the money. She'd tried to buy her way free today, refusing the need he had to take care of her.

The night wore on. Each leaden tick of the neon clock he watched seemed to echo, to mock his own endless, silent screams. Midnight. One A.M. And then it was two, the latest hour she'd ever come home.

The anticipation that she might yet show surged through him. The dread that she wouldn't had him running down twenty flights of stairs, then back up.

Winded, he returned to the loft and positioned a chair near the door. Before sitting, he flicked off the lights. The better to see the neon clock's face, the generous pie slice of illuminated hands calling it three. And then four.

This was worse than limbo; he was in hell.

Aaron was working his gold band like a merry-go-round whipped by a monster tornado when he heard the click of a latch. A glance at the neon clock: 4:19 A.M.

Was that all? He could have sworn she'd been gone more than a year. Lord knew he'd aged ten in a matter of hours.

His eyes adjusted to the dark, he saw her slip in and make a beeline for her room, where her clothes hung but where she no longer slept.

Aaron surged from his post and stole behind her. He didn't touch her, fearful that he'd try to shake every secret out of her head. But he couldn't keep silent and snarled in a seething accusation:

"You were out when I called to apologize. I'm way past that now, so screw the lies. You tell me—and I mean *now*—where you were when you weren't at the club. But first things first:

"Just who the hell were you with?"

NINETEEN

Though he did not touch her, his words hit at her back like cruel blows.

"Go to bed, Aaron," she said in a steely voice. "Just go to bed and don't wake up until I'm out of your suffocating, suspicious reach."

Hurrying on, she could hear his footfall nipping at her heels, the sound of his harsh breathing too close behind her mingling with the sound of her own rapid heartbeat.

The dark was her ally, masking her face and the raw emotions she couldn't hide. She went to her closet and by feel found a large shopping bag. Quickly, she began to rifle through her wardrobe for a few clothes, *her* clothes, to take with her. Where to, she didn't know. All she knew was that she had to get away for a while, to lick her wounds that Aaron had so meanly inflicted.

"Were you with another man?" His voice was amazingly soft, frighteningly calm.

Addy yanked a dress off a satin hanger. Realizing it was her cancan dress, she flung her most beloved piece of clothing in his direction.

"That's yours," she hissed. "Keep it."

"*You're mine*. And I *keep* what is mine."

"Can't keep what you don't own." She moved to her vanity dresser and frantically rummaged through her jewelry box to find the things he'd given her. Something that felt like a black fog of gathering doom filled the air behind her. Aaron stood much too close, but he didn't touch her. Slowly turning, she took his hand and could feel he was shaking. She shook, too, in fury, in hurt. One by one, Addy laid in his palm earrings, necklace, watch. And then she firmly folded his fingers over them.

"I belong to myself, Aaron. Not you."

Clink. Clink. Clink. The sound of stones and pearls hitting the marble floor could have passed for bitter tears rained from the sky and onto a tin roof.

"Then you *were* with another man today, weren't you?" Any tears she thought she might have heard in his whisper were blown away by his roar: "Answer me, dammit!"

"Yes!" she shouted back. "It was just him and me, and I loved every second we spent together!"

Aaron made a garbled, horrible noise that sounded as if he was choking, and then he was groaning, "Oh God, oh God," and she felt sick with the knowledge that she had hurt him so. But he had wounded her just as deep.

What had been a sharp cut she was nursing when she arrived home had become a laceration that gaped wider with each accusation.

But this—Aaron actually believing her capable of stepping out on him—was a betrayal in itself. It was the worst thing he'd ever said or done to her, a devastating blow.

He fell silent, his pain so palpable, she could feel it mingle with hers. Her heart yearned to comfort him, forgive him. Her arms ached to hold him tight while she professed her innocence of such an unthinkable crime. She hugged herself in misery and thus managed not to touch him, console him with the truth. It was a more important truth she confronted him with.

"You didn't trust me," she whispered. "Trust and love, Aaron, they go hand in hand."

"Trust?" His laugh was jagged. "Now there's a concept. Especially coming from a wife who lied to me so she could cheat on me." He was breathing hard, and she could hear the strike of his fist into his palm. "So tell me"—*smack*,—"just how happy,"—*smack*—"does he keep you?"

SMACK! She felt more than saw the silhouette of Aaron's face rock back as she slapped him while the sound echoed in her ears as if she'd struck several blows, not one. Her palm stung, but she welcomed the tingling pain that was more real than this living nightmare spinning out of control.

Aaron laughed an ugly sound. And then he howled as if the demons of the dark were unleashed in a single mad pack.

But even more ominous was his sudden silence. Silence he broke with a devastating softness, like the prick of a fork into the yolk of an egg.

"I'm turning the other cheek. Go ahead, hit me again. Better yet, why don't I give you one of my sculpting knives to cut what you haven't already torn out of my chest? My heart, Addy. Feel it."

He grabbed her hand and pressed her palm there, making her feel too much.

"You say without trust there can't be love. That's not completely true. What trust I had, you destroyed tonight. But the love's still there—it always will be, damn you."

She could hear his teeth grinding as if he was fighting for control, and then the hard swallow of it going down. "I can't let you leave. Wherever you were, whoever you were with, it doesn't matter. I told you to spread your wings with my blessing, said you were my lover, not my wife. But you are, Addy. *You are my wife.* Your place is with me, not with Tony or any other man, ever. That's just the way it is, and how it's always going to be."

"Tony?" she whispered, feeling as if a thief had robbed her as she slept, falsely secure in the haven of dreams while her most cherished possessions were plundered and violated. She could feel herself quake, threatening to erupt all over the place.

"How do you know about Tony?" she demanded.

"How do you think?" he said, at least having the decency to sound as if he was feeling some little guilt.

"So you were following me. How could you do it, Aaron?"

"Easy. I was worried about your safety, and I wanted to be there to protect you if need be."

"But surely you realized that I was fine. Seems that the only protection I needed was from you."

His sigh was tinged with disgust. "Look, I'm not proud of letting my insecurities get the better of me. But let's face it, they turned out to be valid."

"They weren't before, but they are now. You see, when I came home tonight, I hoped that you'd be asleep and I could sneak into my old bed so I could rest up before we had the fight I knew we were sure to have. Oh, yes, I was mad about all your calls to check up on my whereabouts, but I wasn't mad enough to leave you. That was before you falsely accused me, acting like everything we've shared is a lie."

Addy made a long reach for the bedside lamp. "I've never given you any reason to distrust me. Only, it wasn't just me you did damage to, it was us."

A press of her thumb, and the light was on.

Aaron's mouth went slack in mute horror. And then he blinked. Again and again. And then he rubbed his eyes as though he couldn't believe what he was seeing. While he was speechless, Addy was quick to drive home her point.

"I've always loved you, Aaron, though right now for the life of me, I can't understand why. Almost five years ago you left me, and I reckon you had just cause. But still I believed you'd come back and loved you as my very own fairy-tale hero. Even after you warned me that you couldn't live up to my imaginings and proved it several times over, I never stopped loving you. I never quit trusting you, believing in you."

Had he heard her? His eyes mirrored shock, and he was groaning, "Your hair. Your hair, your hair . . ."

"So there it is, the difference between your love and mine," she rushed on to say. "With plenty of temptation on either side of the rope, trust and love are sure to win the tug-of-war every time. You should have let me go without a qualm, because if your heart had been as true as mine, it would've told you all along that I'd come home to stay and never leave."

Unable to bear his horrified stare a moment longer, she picked up her bag and said plainly, "After tonight, I need to leave and think on all this awhile. When I'm done thinking and licking my wounds, I'll be back. Do us both a favor and don't try to find me. Do us a better favor. *Trust me.* Trust me to come back."

Aaron was suddenly blocking the two pillars to her room, bracing them as if he were Sampson on a rampage.

"*How could you do it?*"

It was an accusation almost as incisive as his others and certainly more cutting than the scissors that Bruce had carefully used to cut her hair. Poor Bruce—she could still hear him begging her to stop at her shoulders. By the time he shaved her neck, he was weeping.

"Your hair, your hair," Aaron repeated.

"That's right, *my* hair."

Addy touched the wispy strands at her temples, still unsure if she liked it herself. But Aaron's reaction was one of such horror that she cringed. Did she really look so awful? Only pride kept her from begging him to tell her that she was still beautiful to him, even if it was a lie.

Realizing that her chin had begun to tremble, she lifted it defiantly.

"It was my hair to cut, not yours. Just as our lives together are *our* lives, not yours to manipulate to your own advantage!"

"*Your hair*," he repeated, grabbing at his own as if he could make hers reappear by proxy. "How could you do such a thing? Such a sin, such . . . Who did this? Tell me the name, dammit! I'm going to break the hand that did this to you!"

"Then break mine. If someone else hadn't done it, I would have done it myself."

He clutched at the pillars as if to keep from grabbing her and shaking her until her hair grew back.

"You knew, *you knew*, how much I loved your hair," he finally said with a measure of control. "Why did you do it? Was it to spite me? I mean, this is no small trim to your shoulders. You made a statement, loud and clear."

"Well, you've certainly made a few of your own tonight. The hair can grow back. Lots sooner than you can mend the damage you've done."

"Damage?" he repeated softly. "*Damage*. Lady, you've no idea what you've been doing to me all these years."

"Me? What have I ever done to you?"

"Where to start, where to start . . . Oh, did I ever mention that for four years I kept my eyes shut whenever I was in bed with a woman so I could pretend she was you? And that's not even counting the guilt I lived with, wanting a girl who had the body of a woman. I thought I was some kind of pervert. I went to a shrink for help, but talking about you only made my 'fixation' worse."

When she could only stare at him, stunned, and perversely pleased, Aaron snorted. "I can see by the satisfied look on your face that you don't feel a bit of guilt for the harm done to my mental, not to mention emotional, stability. So I won't hold my breath for any sympathy in the matter of my career."

"What! I have posed for you when I was dead on my feet and kept you going when you were dead on yours. And you want sympathy from me? The hell! I have given you nothing but support."

"I never would've needed your support if you hadn't done such a number on me in that barn. Dreams, Addy, did I ever tell you about my dreams?"

"What dreams?" she asked, unsure if she wanted to know.

"Oh, not just any dreams, believe me. Vivid, technicolor erotic dreams that weren't satisfied with visiting me in sleep. They found their way into my every waking hour until the dreams ended up in my work. Simplistic rural settings and bright colors? I couldn't see them anymore. All I could see was your face, your soul, your body reaching out to me. And wrapped around us, what did I see? *Your hair*."

He took an uneven breath, then shouted, "And it's gone! I can understand why you'd want to get back at me, but *this*—this is too much."

It was hard to sympathize with a screaming brute who was acting as if he loved her hair more than her. When Addy found her voice, it came with a teeth-gritting fury.

"Why do I get this awful feeling that you could've dealt with me cheating on you easier than me cutting off my hair? Oh, yes, I know the darn stuff *inspires* you, and—" She smacked her forehead. "Now I get it! In all that muttering, obsessed sculpting of yours, what do I see most? The hair! You've got a hair"—she had to think, then found the word—"fetish. Well, it's gone now, and all your ranting and raving's not gonna make it grow back. It's gone, Aaron." She ducked under his arm. "And so am I."

His hand shot out, and he jerked her back.

"Just where the hell do you think you're going?"

"Not that it's any of your business, but I have no idea. All I know is that I've got some thinking to do, and I can't think straight when I'm with you. Let go."

"*You* let go." He was fighting her for ownership of the flimsy clothes bag, and once he had it, he threw it somewhere in the dark loft. A resounding thud was followed by a loud crash.

Thinking fast, Addy said, "Aaron! What if you knocked down one of your finished pieces? Lord, I hope it's not my favorite and—and please, let me go check."

She broke free and shot straight for the front door.

The slam of his fist against the cracked exit blended with her rapid pants, his blue profanities, and the sound of locks as he efficiently slipped them into place.

"You're *not* leaving. I won't allow it."

"And just who do you think you are, thinking you can stop me?"

"Your husband, that's who. And *you* are my wife, who is staying here for as long as it takes you to realize that I'm not about to let you walk out on our vows. For better or worse, richer or poorer, till death do us part. You said it, I said it, and that's that."

"No, it's not. I need some room to breathe so I can think while you learn the value of trust."

"I'll learn it, but you're stuck with me while I do. Running away doesn't solve anything, Addy. You're not running away. You're staying, like it or not." He put his face in hers and whispered, *"Wife."*

It was a hot, intimate whisper filled with overtones of demand, command, and possession. Gone was any pretense of the polished, civilized man of the world, Aaron was insistently pushing her from the door. It was a dark stranger who was stalking her like a primitive, rough-hewn man of the mountains. The core of him unveiled, Addy was startled to realize that the dark stranger was no stranger but a man she knew too well.

Aaron *was* the reigning clansman, the Breedlove most high. And she was the wife he expected to bend to his ironclad rule. As he backed her deeper into the loft, the raw power he exuded made her heart pound, her blood run cold and hot all at once. How blind she'd been, unable to see the forest for the trees. For all their clashes and coziness Aaron had never once shared the reins; he'd only let her *think* the spitting kitten could hold her own with an old tom.

He pursued her with such single-minded purpose

that she clutched for something, anything, to steady her unsteady legs and turned over a sculpture.

Aaron kicked aside the biggest pieces before his boots stomped over the shattered remains.

Frantic, Addy demanded, "Who says we're married besides some relatives and a preacher that are holed up in the foothills?"

"Who says? *Me. Me* and a ring on my finger that matches the one on yours."

Goaded by desperation, the utter need to breathe— *Lord, she couldn't even breathe*—to run as fast as she could from this stalking force unleashed, she pulled off her ring and threw it at him.

"There. There you go, we're not married! My ring's gone, Aaron, and the state of New York's not about to support some Appalachian vows that're bound by a mountain, not outsider laws."

"As of now, I *am* the law. Get used to the idea—the honeymoon's over, and the real marriage is at hand."

Before she could dart, he lunged and hauled her over one massive shoulder. Over her screams he bellowed, "You can get rid of the ring, but you can't get rid of me. Now that we've got that settled, forget any fighting for the time being, we'll finish it later. I *am* your husband, Addy Breedlove. And right now your husband is ready to claim his husbandly rights."

He tossed her off his shoulder onto . . . her bed.

Gasping for breath, she watched him strip off his shirt. He reached for his belt, then stopped. Legs braced wide, he folded his arms as if he were the king of Siam.

Or the proud owner of a mountain and a woman he claimed as his.

"I'll leave the rest," he said, "so my wife can do the honors. And after we're officially through consummating our marriage—which shouldn't take much more than a week—you'll have to find that ring yourself and ask me to put it back on. And you will, Addy. *You will.* Just as you'll repeat your vows all over again at the local courthouse— a second time for good measure."

She folded her hands tightly on clasped knees and defied him as much as she dared. "If you're expecting me to 'do the honors,' you'll be waiting a lot more than a week."

The amused lift of his brow and his low chuckle were so infuriating that her pulse jumped with a welcome simmer of anger. That he actually expected to bed her after their horrible scene, after scaring the living day- lights out of her, and hadn't so much as apologized for his nasty words and behavior—well!

"That belt of yours can molder of old age before I'll so much as touch it," she informed him, her nose high in the air.

"Care to make a wager?" Aaron checked his watch. "I'd be willing to bet one of your paychecks and groceries for a month that you'll have my belt *and* pants off in fifteen minutes. If they stay on a minute longer, you have the satisfaction of paying your way. If not, you'll have a husband on your hands who's satisfying you with a vengeance."

"And just what kind of wager is *that*?"

"A very generous one, Mrs. Breedlove. Either way you can't lose. Like I said earlier today, you're lucky to have me. And believe me, you *will* have me. Trust me, it's true."

Addy eyed him warily as he dropped his watch onto the nightstand, and then he was looking at her with a hot, liquid stare that made her shiver with desire and toasted her very toes. Just when she expected him to pounce, he cut a lazy path to her vanity and returned with two intimate weapons that had her scrambling for the safety of the bed's far side.

As he had on their first wedding night, he grabbed her by the ankle, pulling her back. With the concentration of a man bent on a mission, he deflected her kicking heels and in next to no time had her shoes and fishnet hose off.

He stilled her frantic fists with a deft wrap of fishnet stockings around her wrists. He anchored the top portion to the headboard of black iron.

"No! It's not fair, stop—stop—"

"Whoever said I was fair? Certainly not me, babe. But don't worry, I'll let you loose soon enough. Can't do those honors without your hands free," he said smoothly, and just as smoothly he got rid of her bustier with a jerk. Next went the black leather skirt. Despite her struggles she noticed he glanced at the watch. And smiled.

And then he was crouched over her, tossing up his first weapon of choice and catching it neatly. So, it was to be the powder puff and *then* the blush brush.

"Your nose looks a bit shiny to me. Think I'll start

there." He stilled her thrashing head with a span of fingers that reached from her temple to her chin.

"Stop—"

An upward lift of her face, and he silenced her mouth with his lips while he softly brushed her cheek with the puff. After giving the same attention to the other, he dabbed at the moisture he'd left on her lips.

"I do love your lips," he murmured, patting and caressing her neck, then slowly moving down as he tortured her even more sweetly with his words. "I love how your lips fit with mine, the way they open to let your tongue slip into my mouth, or to take whatever I have to offer. I even love them when they're giving me hell. And I love them when they make me smile. It's no wonder you make me go a little crazy, so crazy that I'm jealous of any man who looks at you. But I want them to envy me. Me, the chosen son who chose himself the most maddening, riveting wife any man could ever have."

He plied the powder puff with unerring accuracy. A backward reach and he tickled the undersides of her knees, stroked the insides of her thighs.

"I know it must be hard—by the way, it seems I'm always hard for you, even when I work, but I'm harder now than I've ever been—anyway, where was I?" She moaned as he began to fluff circles around her breasts and then tapped her nipples lightly until they were puckered and hard.

"Oh, yes," he murmured, "I'm so very sorry for those accusations that I'd sell my soul to take them back. But those words are said and done, and the best I can hope for is making things right. Do you think you could forgive me, even just a little, if I told you how crazy in love I am with my wife?"

His eyes were a searing touch, complementing and competing with his sensitive strokes of the delicate fluff. Tossing the powder puff away, he twirled the makeup brush around as if it were a tiny baton and proceeded to sweep it over her upper lip and then her forehead.

"You're sweating. I've been sweating bullets since you almost seduced me in Papa's barn. But that night you took the stage, you were so such a natural, so absolutely amazing that I couldn't stand to listen, to look. I was afraid—afraid of losing you, of not being enough for you. I'm only human, Addy. So human that I doubted you because I doubted myself more. I was scared. *Terrified* that I couldn't keep you. And so I held too tight."

He held her bucking hips still and said with a quiet passion, "I know myself too well, Addy. Even when I'm pushing ninety and you're a wrinkled great-great-grandmother yourself, I'll still be making demands, demanding to hold the rainbow that you are and always will be. You see, Addy, you did a wonderful, terrible thing. You made me believe in dreams."

His hands were desperate and seemed to be everywhere at once, caressing her neck and her hair.

"Untie me," she begged. "Let the damn things loose so I can touch you. Dear God, *let me touch you.*"

"What do you want to touch?"

"Your face, your soul, everywhere. But—but I'll start with your belt." As he made short work of the bindings, she glanced at the nightstand and asked with what little breath she had, "What time is it?"

"Who the hell cares?" The hose untied, he threw the watch across the room, then kissed her with a ravenous passion. Her hands fumbled fast and furious with his belt, his pants, while he pressed his lips to her ear. "Your money's as good as mine. If we're still alive by the time we get out of this bed, how do you feel about opening a joint account?"

"That's the most romantic suggestion you've ever made," she sighed as his tongue ran down her body, painting her with sweeping strokes of emotion and demand.

"Does that mean that you forgive me?" he asked, looking up from her navel, then returning to explore its indentation.

It was a lot to forgive, yet forgive him she did. But there was something else still unresolved, and that was the matter of trust. Her trust in Aaron was complete, almost. What she didn't trust was his trust in her.

It had been shaken so easily. What guarantees did she have that he believed in her enough never to doubt her again?

"I forgive you," was all she said.

As was Aaron's way, enough wasn't enough. He pressed a kiss to the juncture of her thighs, and once he'd had his way with her there, he kissed his way back up. His face impassioned, he beseeched her, "Say that you are my wife."

He loomed large as a mountain above her, larger than the mountain they shared. She envisioned that faraway mountain encircled by a pair of gold rings, Aaron's rimming the earthy base while her own rode halfway to the top. The man who would be king was offering his all and yet no equal share of his throne. He wanted her on his lap.

Addy carefully chose her words.

"I will be your wife, Aaron. Never doubt it."

"You *are* my wife."

She was much too desirous, too greedy, for the feel of his strength to clarify the difference between his statement and her promise.

"Sure you want me, even with my short hair?"

"I love your hair," he murmured, playing with it.

"That's a lie, but I'll take it just the same."

"No lie. I'll always love your hair, long or short. Because as much as I want to get tangled up in it and never find my way back, it's you—all of you—that I want. Yesterday, today, forever."

Her heart broke a little at hearing those words. Today was today, but tomorrow was tomorrow. She dreaded its coming already. So she clung to him even more fiercely, wrapped her willow-strong legs around his thighs, and begged him, "Come home to me. Be inside me where you belong."

"That I do." She felt the intimate rub of his ring. "Mrs. Breedlove, your husband is eager to come home, never to leave. Home is where the heart is. My heart, Addy, it's yours. It always has been, it always will be. Take me. Take me home and share your life with me."

He plunged so deep that she gasped at the totality of his claiming. She fed his insatiable hunger while he stoked hers higher with each reluctant retreat, each eager return home.

In all their past intimacies they had never made love like this. He was a madman possessed. She was a wild woman clawing and begging for his possession without a stitch of pride. Neither of them had any use for pride now as they stripped each other bare until their souls were as naked as their bodies.

What they shared was tenderly human and inhumanly raw. It was pagan and holy. Artless and eloquent in its primitive grace

They were a tangle of limbs sliding over mingled sweat when he lifted her hips high and made his final, claiming plunge with the shout of *"My wife."*

By now they were on the floor, and there they lay for a very long time. With the sun shining, he vowed quietly, fiercely, "I love you, Addy Breedlove."

She gazed from him to the ceiling where a painted, winking half-moon smiled. "And I love you, Aaron Breedlove." She pressed down his droopy eyelids. Kissing one, then the other, she said softly, "Go to sleep."

Aaron granted her the pretense of it. Hard as it was, he made his grip go lax. And as he knew that she would, Addy slipped from his arms. He let her go because he knew Addy as well as he knew himself.

Addy needed him to trust her to come back. As for himself, he needed to put his own demons to rest before he could grant her that trust.

TWENTY

Through the slits of his eyes he watched her put on her cancan dress. He stifled a pleased smile when she girded herself with the heavy artillery of rubies and pearls, gold and diamonds, around her neck and wrist and clipped the grace notes onto her ears.

He tensed and forced himself to remain quiet as she left the room, glad that he had when she returned with the shopping bag and something else that she placed on the vanity. She picked up the antique brush and put it in the bag, along with several changes of clothes.

She left again and returned to cover him with a drop cloth. But not just any drop cloth; it was the one they'd first made love on.

Next she rummaged in her purse and laid a check and a stack of bills on the nightstand. Aaron quelled the urge to ask if she'd kept enough to tide her over.

And then he saw her twist open a tube of bright red

lipstick and write her parting message on the vanity mirror.

He shut his eyes tightly and prayed for the strength to remain silent as she softly touched her lips to his.

"I love you, Aaron, love you ever so much. Try to understand that I'm not really gone—I'm as close as your heart. And you can always touch me—you do it each minute you work." The last she choked out, and it was the hardest thing he'd ever done not to hold her to him and assure her that he understood, that one day they'd finally get it right.

But they would do it Addy's way. He'd had his say; this time it was her turn to have the last word. Give and take, that's what marriage was all about. It was just a lot easier said than done.

Though his heart was hammering, he remained stone-still until he heard the distant catch of a dead bolt.

He got up, and his limbs were so exhausted that he was amazed she'd had the physical strength to make it to her feet, much less down to the street. But then again, Addy had a wellspring of strength to match his and more.

What had it cost her to leave her wedding ring on the vanity? Dearly, he had no doubt.

Turning his attention to the lipsticked message, he read aloud, "Wear it. Trust me."

Aaron wiped a tear from his cheek and drew a heart with an arrow through it beneath her message.

Addy's wedding band hung on a gold chain around his neck. Despite his effort with lotion and soap, it wasn't going past the knuckle of his pinkie, and so he wore it as close to his heart as he could get it.

He moved Addy's vanity into his studio. He looked at her lipsticked message whenever he felt his trust slipping, but he looked less and less as his endless, work-filled days trudged on. Perhaps Papa was with him, helping him be strong, or perhaps the chosen son was determined to prove his trust in the loyalty of his chosen wife.

No doubt a lot of both. On better days he laughed at the thought of Papa and Addy joining forces to bring him to a higher plane of understanding. On the bad days he cursed them both along with himself and took to the stairs with the chant: "A more perfect mate you'll never meet. God, get her home fast so she can stomp her high heels on my clay feet."

Amazingly, he did some of his best work in her absence. And amazingly, the work he was most proud of was an echo from the past, a primitive art piece. It was the only place he could embrace her, translate memory into reality. His misery was eating him up, and yet it was transcendent, working a calming magic on the dregs of doubt and anxiety.

He'd given in to that doubt once, early on, and called the club knowing full well she wasn't there. He did it on the pretense of making excuses for Addy, should she be in breach of contract.

No contract. It turned out Addy had insisted on a handshake and half of what she'd been offered. Aaron had wanted to shout, he was bursting with such pride. But in his heart he knew he should be nodding without surprise. Addy would never prostitute what she freely gave. Addy never had been, never would be, for sale.

Though she'd called in to tell them to find another singer, no other singer would do. Mort was playing Bach, and that didn't exactly bring the customers in droves when they'd come to hear Addy. *Where was she?*

Aaron was 99 percent sure that he knew. But he wasn't about to betray her trust with the information he refused to act on himself.

Instead, he'd advised them, "Trust her. She'll be back. Just be sure you save the best seat for her husband. *Me.*"

Opening night.

Would Addy show? She knew the date, the importance of it. Time was running on empty for her to grace the milling crowd with her presence, the very presence that had inspired him to pay tribute to a woman no man could hold.

He had let her go. Stupidity? Wisdom? Both.

In all his showings he'd kept an anxious count of what sold, what didn't, and held his breath until the art critics raved once more. But now, with the stakes so high he should be queasy, Aaron found himself wishing that he wouldn't sell a single work. He wanted to keep them all for himself. But that wouldn't be right. Addy was the essence of life; she was meant to be shared.

As the night wore on, card after card was placed on life-sized piece after piece, declaring them sold. All but two.

Trying to make himself as invisible as possible, Aaron gave his back to the critics and collectors and touched the lips of the sculpture, begging for a kiss.

"They're asking me to point you out, Aaron." James placed a hand on his shoulder.

"Tell them I ducked out, temperamental artist that I am."

"It would seem that you're in a fine temper, and I know the reason why. Where's Addy?"

"Take a look around. She's everywhere."

James tapped the Not for Sale card. "Everywhere but here is more like it. Why don't you go after her?"

"Because I trust her. It's as complex and as simple as that. Any more questions?"

"Well . . . yes. I have two. First of all, I could have sold this piece two dozen times over. Would you do us both a financial favor and consider letting some copies go in a limited edition? Surely, you still have the mold."

"Sorry, but I broke the mold. This piece is one of a kind, and it's not for sale. Just like Addy. Next question?"

James cleared his throat. "What you've done here is as wonderful as Addy, and I can understand now why you were so driven. But that doesn't explain why you turned primitive art on its head ten years ago, turned your back on it, and *voilà* here you are, doing it all over again. What in God's name possessed you to do such a thing? How could you turn out the best piece of primitive art you've ever done, let it be known you'll never work in that style again, and refuse to sell your last and most unforgettable masterpiece?"

Aaron chuckled. "Beginnings and endings, James, they've got a lot in common. Addy brought me full circle. Let's leave it at that."

Suddenly, Aaron felt something pressing in and getting closer. But that something was too familiar, too divine and heady, to doubt with the turn of his head. And so he continued to stare at the hanging sculpture with pink virgin lips. James left with a promise that he'd ward off the remains of the salivating pack while Aaron made his peace with the demon that had driven him to the heights of heaven, the bowels of hell.

"Sure is a fine picture sculpture you've got here, Aaron Breedlove. A cut above the rest and those are all sold. Think you could be generous enough to sell this one to me?"

"Nothing to sell, Addy. Everything I have is already yours for the keeping."

He turned in slow motion. Even more slowly Addy lifted a bare left hand to her shoulder and released the frayed white tie to the sundress she'd worn when she nearly seduced him on a haystack in Papa's barn. How she'd grown.

But thanks to Addy, so had he.

Aaron's gaze lowered to her shoes. She wore a pair of worn-out boots, the sole coming apart from the shoe leather. Even with the polished tips of his shoes touching hers, there was no poverty to be found between them. They were rich, so very rich, in their understanding and love of each other.

Aaron devoured her with his gaze while he jerked a button off his shirt and pressed it into her palm.

"Lord, but it must be a pearl," she murmured, then kissed it before tucking the button into the haven of her bodice.

"More priceless than pearls," he assured her, "is trust."

"That's a fact. Here I am, and here I'll always be. Wherever you are, I'll be there too." She fingered the gold ring that hung from his neck. "Will you put it on my finger where it belongs?"

Unlatching the chain, Aaron freed the ring and poised it at the tip of Addy's finger. Though his need to slide it down to its rightful place was great, he hesitated.

Gripping the ring, he pocketed it. "I'll put it on in front of a judge. But I have an early wedding present for you, one that's been a long time coming."

"But besides you, what gift could you give me?"

Smiling mysteriously, he led her to where it all started. Extending his hand to his labor of love, Aaron said, "Welcome home."

Quick tears sprang to her eyes. The dollhouse she beheld was far finer than any mansion on a glossy magazine page. She touched the tin roof, then ran her fingertip down to the rough wood porch. Peering inside, she saw her life as she'd once known it. Within the dollhouse there was no microwave, no telephone, no fancy furniture.

There was, however, a potbellied stove and a table set for a family. Two carved fireplaces, seeming to be put to good use, fire leaping up from charred, weathered wood. Two tiny bedrooms jutted off from the homey but sparse parlor. One had a crib in it, an itsy-bitsy crocheted blanket thrown over the side. A miniature oil lamp graced the side of a feather-bed mattress in the other bedroom. She stuck her finger in through an open window and touched the seat of an intricately carved rocker.

When she let go, the chair began to rock back and forth.

"I want to go home," she whispered.

"Now that you're here, we're both already there." She fell into his arms, and he sealed that truth with a hungry kiss of reunion. "Truce?" he asked.

"Truce." Addy's kiss-swollen lips curved into a Mona Lisa smile. "A truce bound in trust. Mind if Tony stands up with me at the courthouse since Loretta's not here?"

"Tell you what. You can have Tony so long as you agree to honeymoon in Half-moon Hollow."

"I wouldn't have it any other way. Oh, and by the way, I told all the folks we were very happily married."

"In that case you told the truth." Aaron swept her into his arms. Then, at the gallery's doors, he spied a polished black Bentley.

"Well, what are we waiting for?" she asked impatiently.

"Only the best for my wife." At the raise of his finger, their driver was as good as there.

Aaron greeted him with a conspiratorial wink and a formal request of "Home, James."

EPILOGUE

There is a place that goes by the name of Half-moon Hollow. And within that hidden pocket of time in Appalachia, there exists little modern civilization and yet a wealth of truth.

"I learned my lesson, Addy McDonald Breedlove."

Embracing him upon his ancestor's bed that they shared on this, their first anniversary, Addy luxuriated in the feel of his arms around her. Pulling her lips from the possessive hold of his, she wrinkled her nose and inquired tartly, "Did you now, oh great chosen son who chose me for a wife? Two times over, just to make sure."

"That I did. Bit off almost more than I could chew, but then again, so did you."

"Must run in the family." They shared a good laugh and an even better kiss. "I think Loretta's giving Jonas hell."

"Then she must love him enough to let him off easy. God knows that hell has nothing on you."

"I'll take that as a compliment." While she stroked Aaron's back, he played with the uncut ends of her hair that she'd decided to let grow because she missed the feel of his hands twining in it. "Speaking of Jonas and Loretta, it greatly pleases me that they're agreeable to tending the mountain for us."

"Me too." Aaron shook his head. "But how much longer before the outside claims it from McDonalds and Breedloves alike?"

Addy waved her hand in front of his distant gaze. "Wake up, Aaron. The mountain's no more than a heap of piled dirt and big trees. But real love grows and grows and has no more pride than reason. Love simply is, and that's all there is to it."

"I reckon you're right," he agreed. "But it makes me sad that the elders are dying and the young people are laying to rest the traditions that got us together. I'm afraid our children will surely think we're telling fairy tales about a time and place that should never die, along with its truths."

"But every fairy tale has a truth at its core. They'll find those truths, Aaron, as well as their roots that can never die even long after we're dead."

"Do you really believe that? If you do, I'll put aside reason and believe in our future."

Addy snorted. "Here you go again, wanting to put the past behind us while you can't stand to let it go. Did I ever tell you that you tend to talk out of both sides of your mouth?"

"Leave it to you to remind me." He tucked a friendship quilt up to their nuzzling chins. "Whichever way I talked or thought, I never wanted Half-moon Hollow to die, even when I was desperate to get free of its hold. The hamlet, Addy, it's fading fast. And much as I didn't want to be the chosen son, I wish we had a child that I could pass that honor on to one day."

"Whether that honor gets passed on or not, I found out just before we left that we've got something cooking in the oven." She led his palm to her belly. "Thought I'd save the news for a first anniversary present."

Addy gave a smile to the half-moon winking into the window. Seemed to her that the moon and truces and love had a whole lot in common.

"Are you sure?" Aaron stroked her belly possessively, protectively, and took on a look so proud, he'd surely take to strutting any minute, moonshine bottle in hand.

"Sure as I breathe." Addy winked back at the half-moon. Their hands linked, and gold rode upon gold as she gave Aaron a witchy, sweet smile and said softly, "Trust me."

And trust her he did.

A POSTSCRIPT FROM THE AUTHOR

In the process of scrambling for a unique twist on a gripping romance, I emerged with what I thought was a hat-trick plot: The Hatfields and McCoys meet *My Fair Lady*.

That was *before* I did my research. I discovered that satirizing the Appalachian culture would be tantamount to getting a good laugh at the expense of the homeless. Studies were limited, and those available, dated. What emerged was a tragedy equal to that of the American Indian. Rare riches crowded out by poverty and what we outsiders call progress.

I walk away from this novel with regret for what can't be changed and some shame for my preconceived concepts. Indeed, what few hamlets might be left are dying, as are the skills and way of life they take with them.

Half-moon Hollow has escaped extinction by virtue of its isolation and my imagination.

For those of you who are interested in learning more about this special slice of American heritage, I highly recommend the Foxfire series, available in libraries and bookstores.

But that's fact, and we're lovers of fiction. So . . . do chosen sons and the wives they choose for the sake of a truce really exist? As surely as Romeo and Juliet ever did.

Tragedy and comedy, two sides of the same coin.

Flip the coin just right and wish upon a star with me.

THE EDITOR'S
CORNER

Along with the May flowers come six fabulous Love-swepts that will dazzle you with humor, excitement, and, above all, love. Touching, tender, packed with emotion and wonderfully happy endings, our six upcoming romances are real treasures.

The ever-popular Charlotte Hughes leads things off with **THE DEVIL AND MISS GOODY TWO-SHOES**, LOVESWEPT #684. Kane Stoddard had never answered the dozens of letters Melanie Abercrombie had written him in prison, but her words had kept his spirit alive during the three years he'd been jailed in error—and now he wants nothing more than a new start, and a chance to meet the woman who touched his angry soul. Stunned by the sizzling attraction she feels for Kane, Mel struggles to deny the passionate emotions Kane's touch awakens. No one had ever believed in Kane until Mel's sweet caring makes him dare to taste her innocent lips, makes him hunger to hold her until the sun rises. He can only hope that his fierce loving will vanquish her fear of losing him. Touching and intense, **THE DEVIL AND MISS GOODY TWO-SHOES** is the kind of love story that Charlotte is known and loved for.

This month Terry Lawrence delivers some **CLOSE ENCOUNTERS**, LOVESWEPT #685—but of the romantic kind. Alone in the elevator with his soon-to-be ex-wife, Tony Paretti decides he isn't giving Sara Cohen up without a fight! But when fate sends the elevator plunging ten floors and tosses her into his arms, he seizes his chance—and with breath-stealing abandon embraces the woman he's never stopped loving. Kissing Sara with a savage passion that transcends pain, Tony insists that what they had was too good to let go, that together they are strong enough to face the grief that shattered their marriage. Sara aches to rebuild the bonds of their love but doesn't know if she can trust him with her sorrow, even after Tony confesses the secret hopes that he's never dared to tell another soul. Terry will have you crying and cheering as these two people discover the courage to love again.

Get ready for a case of mistaken identity in **THE ONE FOR ME**, LOVESWEPT #686, by Mary Kay McComas. It was a ridiculous masquerade, pretending to be his twin brother at a business dinner, but Peter Wesley grows utterly confused when his guest returns from the powder room—and promptly steals his heart! She looks astonishingly like the woman he'd dined with earlier, but he's convinced that the cool fire and passionate longing in her bright blue eyes is new and dangerously irresistible. Katherine Asher hates impersonating her look-alike sisters, and seeing Peter makes her regret she'd ever agreed. When he kisses her with primitive yearning, she aches to admit her secret—that she wants him for herself! Once the charade is revealed, Peter woos her with fierce pleasure until she surrenders. She has always taken her happiness last, but is she ready to put her love for him first? **THE ONE FOR ME** is humorous and hot—just too good to resist.

Marcia Evanick gives us a hero who is **PLAYING FOR KEEPS**, LOVESWEPT #687. For the past two years detective Reece Carpenter has solved the fake murder-mystery at the Montgomery clan's annual family reunion, infuriating the beautiful—and competitive—Tennessee Montgomery. But when he faces his tempting rival this time, all he wants to win is her heart! Tennie has come prepared to beat her nemesis if it kills her—but the wild flames in his eyes light a fire in her blood that only his lips can satisfy. Tricked into working as a team, Tennie and Reece struggle to prove which is the better sleuth, but the enforced closeness creates a bigger challenge: to keep their minds on the case when they can't keep their hands off each other! Another keeper from Marcia Evanick.

STRANGE BEDFELLOWS, LOVESWEPT #688, is the newest wonderful romance from Patt Bucheister. John Lomax gave up rescuing ladies in distress when he traded his cop's mean streets for the peace of rural Kentucky, but he feels his resolve weaken when he discovers Silver Knight asleep on his couch! Her sea nymph's eyes brimming with delicious humor, her temptress's smile teasingly seductive, Silver pleads with him to probe a mystery in her New York apartment—and her hunk of a hero is hooked! Fascinated by her reluctant knight, an enigmatic warrior whose pain only she can soothe, Silver wonders if a joyous romp might help her free his spirit from the demons of a shadowy past. He is her reckless gamble, the dare she can't refuse—but she needs to make him understand his true home is in her arms. **STRANGE BEDFELLOWS** is Patt Bucheister at her sizzling best.

And last, but certainly not least, is **NO PROMISES MADE**, LOVESWEPT #689, by Maris Soule. Eric Newman is a sleek black panther of a man who holds Ashley Kehler spellbound, mesmerizing her with a look that strips her bare and caresses her senses, but he could also make her lose control, forget the dreams that drive her . . . and Ashley knows she must resist this seducer who ignites a fever in her blood! Drawn to this golden spitfire who is his opposite in every way, Eric feels exhilarated, intrigued against his will—but devastated by the knowledge that she'll soon be leaving. Ashley wavers between ecstasy and guilt, yet Eric knows the only way to keep his love is to let her go, hoping that she is ready to choose the life that will bring her joy. Don't miss this fabulous story!

Happy reading!

With warmest wishes,

Nita Taublib

Nita Taublib

Associate Publisher

P.S. Don't miss the exciting women's novels from Bantam that are coming your way in May—**DECEPTION**, by Amanda Quick, is the paperback edition of her first *New York Times* bestselling hardcover; **RELENTLESS**, by award-winning author Patricia Potter, is a searing tale of revenge and desire, set in Colorado during the 1870's; **SEIZED BY LOVE**, by Susan Johnson, is a novel of savage passions and dangerous pleasures sweeping from fabulous country estates and hunting lodges to the opulent ballrooms and salons of Russian nobility; and **WILD CHILD**, by bestselling author Suzanne Forster, reunites adversaries who share a tangled past—and for whom an old spark of conflict will kindle into a dangerously passionate blaze. We'll be giving you a sneak peek at these terrific books in next month's LOVESWEPTs. And immediately following this page look for a preview of the exciting romances from Bantam that are *available now*!

Don't miss these exciting books by your
favorite Bantam authors

On sale in March:

DARK PARADISE

by Tami Hoag

WARRIOR BRIDE

by Tamara Leigh

REBEL IN SILK

by Sandra Chastain

Look For

DARK PARADISE

by

Tami Hoag

Here is nationally bestselling author Tami Hoag's most dangerously erotic novel yet, a story filled with heart-stopping suspense and shocking passion . . . a story of a woman drawn to a man as hard and untamable as the land he loves, and to a town steeped in secrets—where a killer lurks.

Night had fallen by the time Mari finally found her way to Lucy's place with the aid of the map Lucy had sent in her first letter. Her "hide-out," she'd called it. The huge sky was as black as velvet, sewn with the sequins of more stars than she had ever imagined. The world suddenly seemed a vast, empty wilderness, and she pulled into the yard of the small ranch, questioning for the first time the wisdom of a surprise arrival. There were no lights glowing a welcome in the windows of the handsome new log house. The garage doors were closed.

She climbed out of her Honda and stretched, feeling exhausted and rumpled. The past two weeks had sapped her strength, the decisions she had made taking chunks of it at a time. The drive up from Sacramento had been accomplished in a twenty-four hour marathon with breaks for nothing more than the bathroom and truck stop burritos, and now the physical strain of that weighed her down like an anchor.

It had seemed essential that she get here as quickly as possible, as if she had been afraid her nerve would give out and she would succumb to the endless dissatisfaction of her life in California if she didn't escape immediately. The wild pendulum her emotions had been riding had left her feeling drained and dizzy. She had counted on falling into Lucy's care the instant she got out of her car, but Lucy didn't appear to be home, and disappointment sent the pendulum swinging downward again.

Foolish, really, she told herself, blinking back the threat of tears as she headed for the front porch. She couldn't have expected Lucy to know she was coming. She hadn't been able to bring herself to call ahead. A call would have meant an explanation of everything that had gone on in the past two weeks, and that was better made in person.

A calico cat watched her approach from the porch rail, but jumped down and ran away as she climbed the steps, its claws scratching the wood floor as it darted around the corner of the porch and disappeared. The wind swept down off the mountain and howled around the weathered outbuildings, bringing with it a sense of isolation and a vague feeling of desertion that Mari tried to shrug off as she raised a hand and knocked on the door.

No lights brightened the windows. No voice called out for her to keep her pants on.

She swallowed at the combination of disappointment and uneasiness that crowded at the back of her throat. Against her will, her eyes did a quick scan of the moon-shadowed ranch yard and the hills beyond. The place was in the middle of nowhere. She had driven through the small town of New Eden and gone miles into the wilderness, seeing no more than two other houses on the way—and those from a great distance.

She knocked again, but didn't wait for an answer before trying the door. Lucy had mentioned wildlife in her few letters. The four-legged, flea-scratching kind.

"Bears. I remember something about bears," she muttered, the nerves at the base of her neck wriggling at the possibility that there were a dozen watching her from the cover of darkness, sizing her up with their beady little eyes while their stomachs growled. "If it's all the same to you, Luce, I'd rather not meet one up close and personal while you're off doing the boot scootin' boogie with some cowboy."

Stepping inside, she fumbled along the wall for a light switch, then blinked against the glare of a dozen small bulbs artfully arranged in a chandelier of antlers. Her first thought was that Lucy's abysmal housekeeping talents had deteriorated to a shocking new low. The place was a disaster area, strewn with books, newspapers, note paper, clothing.

She drifted away from the door and into the great room that encompassed most of the first floor of the house, her brain stumbling to make sense of the contradictory information it was getting. The house was barely a year old, a blend of Western tradition and contemporary architectural touches. Lucy had hired a decorator to capture those intertwined feelings in the interior. But the western watercolor prints on the walls hung at drunken angles. The cushions had been torn from the heavy, overstuffed chairs. The seat of the red leather sofa had been slit from end to end. Stuffing rose up from the wound in ragged tufts. Broken lamps and shattered pottery littered the expensive Berber rug. An overgrown pothos had been ripped from its planter and shredded, and was strung across the carpet like strips of tattered green ribbon.

Not even Lucy was this big a slob.

Mari's pulse picked up the rhythm of fear. "Lucy?" she called, the tremor in her voice a vocal extension of the goosebumps that were pebbling her arms. The only answer was an ominous silence that pressed in on her eardrums until they were pounding.

She stepped over a gutted throw pillow, picked her way around a smashed terra cotta urn and peered into the darkened kitchen area. The refrigerator door was ajar, the light within glowing like the promise of gold inside a treasure chest. The smell, however, promised something less pleasant.

She wrinkled her nose and blinked against the sour fumes as she found the light switch on the wall and flicked it upward. Recessed lighting beamed down on a repulsive mess of spoiling food and spilled beer. Milk puddled on the Mexican tile in front of the refrigerator. The carton lay abandoned on its side. Flies hovered over the garbage like tiny vultures.

"Jesus, Lucy," she muttered, "what kind of party did you throw here?"

And where the hell are you?

The pine cupboard doors stood open, their contents spewed out of them. Stoneware and china and flatware lay broken and scattered. Appropriately macabre place settings for the gruesome meal that had been laid out on the floor.

Mari backed away slowly, her hand trembling as she reached out to steady herself with the one ladder-back chair that remained upright at the long pine harvest table. She caught her full lower lip between her teeth and stared through the sheen of tears. She had worked too many criminal cases not to see this for what it was. The house had been ransacked. The motive could have been robbery or the destruction could have been the aftermath of something else, something uglier.

"Lucy?" she called again, her heart sinking like a stone at the sure knowledge that she wouldn't get an answer.

Her gaze drifted to the stairway that led up to the loft where the bedrooms were tucked, then cut to the telephone that had been ripped from the kitchen wall and now hung by slender tendons of wire.

Her heart beat faster. A fine mist of sweat slicked her palms.

"Lucy?"

"She's dead."

The words were like a pair of shotgun blasts in the still of the room. Mari wheeled around, a scream wedged in her throat right behind her heart. He stood at the other end of the table, six feet of hewn granite in faded jeans and a chambray work shirt. How anything that big could have sneaked up on her was beyond reasoning. Her perceptions distorted by fear, she thought his shoulders rivaled the mountains for size. He stood there, staring at her from beneath the low-riding brim of a dusty black Stetson, his gaze narrow, measuring, his mouth set in a grim, compressed line. His right hand—big with blunt-tipped fingers—hung at his side just inches from a holstered revolver that looked big enough to bring down a buffalo.

WARRIOR BRIDE
by
Tamara Leigh

" . . . a vibrant, passionate love story that captures all the splendor of the medieval era . . . A sheer delight."
—*bestselling author Teresa Medeiros*

After four years of planning revenge on the highwayman who'd stolen her future, Lizanne Balmaine had the blackguard at the point of her sword. Yet something about the onyx-eyed man she'd abducted and taken to her family estate was different—something that made her hesitate at her moment of triumph. Now she was his prisoner . . . and even more than her handsome captor she feared her own treacherous desires.

"Welcome, my Lord Ranulf," she said. " 'Tis a fine day for a duel."

He stared unblinkingly at her, then let a frown settle between his eyes. "Forsooth, I did not expect you to attend this bloodletting," he said. "I must needs remember you are not a lady."

Her jaw hardened. "I assure you I would not miss this for anything," she tossed back.

He looked at the weapons she carried. "And where is this man who would champion your ill-fated cause?" he asked, looking past her.

"Man?" She shook her head. "There is no man."

Ranulf considered this, one eyebrow arched. "You were unable to find a single man willing to die for you, my lady? Not one?"

Refusing to rise to the bait, Lizanne leaned forward, smiling faintly. "Alas, I fear I am so uncomely that none would offer."

"And what of our bargain?" Ranulf asked, suspicion cast upon his voice.

"It stands."

"You think to hold me till your brother returns?" He shifted more of his weight onto his uninjured leg. "Do you forget that I am an unwilling captive, my lady? 'Tis not likely you will return me to that foul-smelling cell." He took a step toward her.

At his sudden movement, the mare shied away, snorting loudly as it pranced sideways. Lizanne brought the animal under control with an imperceptible tightening of her legs.

"Nay," she said, her eyes never wavering. "Your opponent is here before you now."

Ranulf took some moments to digest this, then burst out laughing. As preposterous as it was, a mere woman challenging an accomplished knight to a duel of swords, her proposal truly did not surprise him, though it certainly amused him.

And she was not jesting! he acknowledged. Amazingly, it fit the conclusions he had wrestled with, and finally accepted, regarding her character.

Had she a death wish, then? Even if that spineless brother of hers had shown her how to swing a sword, it was inconceivable she could have any proficiency with such a heavy, awkward weapon. A sling, perhaps, and he mustn't forget a dagger, but a sword?

Slowly, he sobered, blinking back tears of mirth and drawing deep, ragged breaths of air.

She edged her horse nearer, her indignation evident in her stiffly erect bearing. "I find no humor in the situation. Mayhap you would care to enlighten me, Lord Ranulf?"

"Doubtless, you would not appreciate my explanation, my lady."

Her chin went up. "Think you I will not make a worthy opponent?"

"With your nasty tongue, perhaps, but—"

"Then let us not prolong the suspense any longer," she snapped. Swiftly, she removed the sword from its scabbard and tossed it, hilt first, to him.

Reflexively, Ranulf pulled it from the air, his hand closing around the cool metal hilt. He was taken aback as he held it aloft, for inasmuch as the weapon appeared perfectly honed on both its edges, it was not the weighty sword he was accustomed to. Indeed, it felt awkward in his grasp.

"And what is this, a child's toy?" he quipped, twisting the sword in his hand.

In one fluid motion, Lizanne dismounted and turned to face him. "'Tis the instrument of your death, my lord." Advancing, she drew her own sword, identical to the one he held.

He lowered his sword's point and narrowed his eyes. "Think you I would fight a woman?"

"'Tis as we agreed."

"I agreed to fight a man—"

"Nay, you agreed to fight the opponent of my choice. I stand before you now ready to fulfill our bargain."

"We have no such bargain," he insisted.

"Would you break your vow? Are you so dishonorable?"

Never before had Ranulf's honor been questioned. For King Henry and, when necessary, himself, he had fought hard and well, and he carried numerous battle scars to attest to his valor. Still, her insult rankled him.

"'Tis honor that compels me to decline," he

said, a decidedly dangerous smile playing about his lips.

"Honor?" She laughed, coming to an abrupt halt a few feet from him. "Methinks 'tis your injury, coward. Surely, you can still wield a sword?"

Coward? A muscle in his jaw jerked. This one was expert at stirring the remote depths of his anger. "Were you a man, you would be dead now."

"Then imagine me a man," she retorted, lifting her sword in challenge.

The very notion was laughable. Even garbed as she was, the Lady Lizanne was wholly a woman.

"Nay, I fear I must decline." Resolutely, he leaned on the sword. "'Twill make a fine walking stick, though," he added, flexing the steel blade beneath his weight.

Ignoring his quip, Lizanne took a step nearer. "You cannot decline!"

"Aye, and I do."

"Then I will gut you like a pig!" she shouted and leaped forward.

REBEL IN SILK
by
Sandra Chastain

*"Sandra Chastain's characters' steamy relationships
are the stuff dreams are made of."*
—Romantic Times

*Dallas Burke had come to Willow Creek, Wyoming,
to find her brother's killer, and she had no intention of being scared off—not by the roughnecks who
trashed her newspaper office, nor by the devilishly
handsome cowboy who warned her of the violence to
come. Yet she couldn't deny that the tall, sunbronzed
rancher had given her something to think about,
namely, what it would be like to be held in his
steel-muscled arms and feel his sensuous mouth on
hers . . . .*

A bunch of liquored-up cowboys were riding past
the station, shooting guns into the air, bearing down
on the startled Miss Banning caught by drifts in the
middle of the street.

From the general store, opposite where Dallas
was standing, came a figure who grabbed her valise
in one hand and scooped her up with the other, flung her over his shoulder, and stepped onto
the wooden sidewalk beneath the roof over the
entrance to the saloon.

Dallas let out a shocked cry as the horses
thundered by. She might have been run over had
it not been for the man's quick action. Now,
hanging upside down, she felt her rescuer's hand

cradling her thigh in much too familiar a manner.

"Sir, what are you doing?"

"Saving your life."

The man lifted her higher, then, as she started to slide, gave her bottom another tight squeeze. Being rescued was one thing, but this was out of line. Gratitude flew out of her mind as he groped her backside.

"Put me down, you . . . you . . . lecher!"

"Gladly!" He leaned forward, loosened his grip and let her slide to the sidewalk where she landed in a puddle of melted snow and ice. The valise followed with a thump.

"Well, you didn't have to try to break my leg!" Dallas scrambled to her feet, her embarrassment tempering her fear and turning it into anger.

"No, I could have let the horses do it!"

Dallas had never heard such cold dispassion in a voice. He wasn't flirting with her. He wasn't concerned about her injuries. She didn't know why he'd bothered to touch her so intimately. One minute he was there, and the next he had turned to walk away.

"Wait, please wait! I'm sorry to appear ungrateful. I was just startled."

As she scurried along behind him, all she could see was the hat covering his face and head, his heavy canvas duster, and boots with silver spurs set with turquoise. He wasn't stopping.

Dallas reached out and caught his arm. "Now, just a minute. Where I come from, a man at least gives a lady the chance to say a proper thank you. What kind of man are you?"

"I'm cold, I'm thirsty, and I'm ready for a woman. Are you volunteering?"

There was a snickering sound that ran through the room they'd entered. Dallas raised her head and glanced around. She wasn't the only woman in the saloon, but she was the only one wearing all her clothes.

Any other woman might have gasped. But Dallas suppressed her surprise. She didn't know the layout of the town yet, and until she did, she wouldn't take a chance of offending anyone, even these ladies of pleasure. "I'm afraid not. I'm a newspaperwoman, not a . . . an entertainer."

He ripped his hat away, shaking off the glistening beads of melting snow that hung in the jet-black hair that touched his shoulders. He was frowning at her, his brow drawn into deep lines of displeasure; his lips, barely visible beneath a bushy mustache, pressed into a thin line.

His eyes, dark and deep, held her. She sensed danger and a hot intensity.

Where the man she'd met on the train seemed polished and well-mannered, her present adversary was anything but a gentleman. He was a man of steel who challenged with every glance. She shivered in response.

"Hello," a woman's voice intruded. "I'm Miranda. You must have come in on the train."

Dallas blinked, breaking the contact between her and her rescuer. With an effort, she turned to the woman.

"Ah, yes. I did. Dallas Banning." She started to hold out her hand, realized that she was clutching her valise, then lowered it. "I'm afraid I've made rather a mess of introducing myself to Green Willow Creek."

"Well, I don't know about what happened in the street, but following Jake in here might give your reputation a bit of a tarnish."

"Jake?" This was the Jake that her brother Jamie had been worried about.

"Why, yes," Miranda said, "I assumed you two knew each other?"

"Not likely," Jake growled and turned to the bar. "She's too skinny and her mouth is too big for my taste."

"Miss Banning?" Elliott Parnell, the gentleman she'd met on the train, rushed in from the street. "I saw what happened. Are you all right?"

Jake looked up, catching Dallas between him and the furious look he cast at Elliott Parnell.

Dallas didn't respond. The moment Jake had spotted Mr. Elliott, everything in the saloon had seemed to stop. All movement. All sound. For a long endless moment it seemed as if everyone in the room were frozen in place.

Jake finally spoke. "If she's with you and your sodbusters, Elliott, you'd better get her out of here."

Elliot took Dallas's arm protectively. "No, Jake. We simply came in on the same train. Miss Banning is James Banning's sister."

"Oh? The troublemaking newspaper editor. Almost as bad as the German immigrants. I've got no use for either one. Take my advice, Miss Banning. Get on the next train back to wherever you came from."

"I don't need your advice, Mr. Silver."

"Suit yourself, but somebody didn't want your brother here, and my guess is that you won't be any more welcome!"

Dallas felt a shiver of pure anger ripple down her backbone. She might as well make her position known right now. She came to find out the truth and she wouldn't be threatened. "Mr. Silver—"

"Jake! Elliott!" Miranda interrupted, a warning in her voice. "Can't you see that Miss Banning is half-frozen? Men! You have to forgive them," she said, turning to Dallas. "At the risk of further staining your reputation, I'd be pleased to have you make use of my room to freshen up and get dry. That is if you don't mind being . . . here."

"I'd be most appreciative, Miss Miranda," Dallas said, following her golden-haired hostess to the stairs.

Dallas felt all the eyes in the room boring holes in her back. She didn't have to be told where she was and what was taking place beyond the doors on either side of the corridor. If being here ruined her reputation, so be it. She wasn't here to make friends anyway. Besides, a lead to Jamie's murderer was a lot more likely to come from these people than those who might be shocked by her actions.

For just a second she wondered what would have happened if Jake had marched straight up the stairs with her. Then she shook off the impossible picture that thought had created.

She wasn't here to be bedded.

She was here to kill a man.

She just had to find out which one.

And don't miss these spectacular
romances from Bantam Books,
on sale in April:

DECEPTION
by the New York Times bestselling author
Amanda Quick
"One of the hottest and most
prolific writers in romance today . . ."
—*USA Today*

RELENTLESS
by the highly acclaimed author
Patricia Potter
"One of the romance genre's
finest talents . . ."
—*Romantic Times*

SEIZED BY LOVE
by the mistress of erotic historical romance
Susan Johnson
"Susan Johnson is one of the best."
—*Romantic Times*

WILD CHILD
by the bestselling author
Suzanne Forster
"(Suzanne Forster) is guaranteed to steam up
your reading glasses."
—*L.A. Daily News*

OFFICIAL RULES

To enter the sweepstakes below carefully follow all instructions found elsewhere in this offer.

The **Winners Classic** will award prizes with the following approximate maximum values: 1 Grand Prize: $26,500 (or $25,000 cash alternate); 1 First Prize: $3,000; 5 Second Prizes: $400 each; 35 Third Prizes: $100 each; 1,000 Fourth Prizes: $7.50 each. Total maximum retail value of Winners Classic Sweepstakes is $42,500. Some presentations of this sweepstakes may contain individual entry numbers corresponding to one or more of the aforementioned prize levels. To determine the Winners, individual entry numbers will first be compared with the winning numbers preselected by computer. For winning numbers not returned, prizes will be awarded in random drawings from among all eligible entries received. Prize choices may be offered at various levels. If a winner chooses an automobile prize, all license and registration fees, taxes, destination charges and, other expenses not offered herein are the responsibility of the winner. If a winner chooses a trip, travel must be complete within one year from the time the prize is awarded. Minors must be accompanied by an adult. Travel companion(s) must also sign release of liability. Trips are subject to space and departure availability. Certain black-out dates may apply.

The following applies to the sweepstakes named above:

No purchase necessary. You can also enter the sweepstakes by sending your name and address to: P.O. Box 508, Gibbstown, N.J. 08027. Mail each entry separately. Sweepstakes begins 6/1/93. Entries must be received by 12/30/94. Not responsible for lost, late, damaged, misdirected, illegible or postage due mail. Mechanically reproduced entries are not eligible. All entries become property of the sponsor and will not be returned.

Prize Selection/Validations: Selection of winners will be conducted no later than 5:00 PM on January 28, 1995, by an independent judging organization whose decisions are final. Random drawings will be held at 1211 Avenue of the Americas, New York, N.Y. 10036. Entrants need not be present to win. Odds of winning are determined by total number of entries received. Circulation of this sweepstakes is estimated not to exceed 200 million. All prizes are guaranteed to be awarded and delivered to winners. Winners will be notified by mail and may be required to complete an affidavit of eligibility and release of liability which must be returned within 14 days of date on notification or alternate winners will be selected in a random drawing. Any prize notification letter or any prize returned to a participating sponsor, Bantam Doubleday Dell Publishing Group, Inc., its participating divisions or subsidiaries, or the independent judging organization as undeliverable will be awarded to an alternate winner. Prizes are not transferable. No substitution for prizes except as offered or as may be necessary due to unavailability, in which case a prize of equal or greater value will be awarded. Prizes will be awarded approximately 90 days after the drawing. All taxes are the sole responsibility of the winners. Entry constitutes permission (except where prohibited by law) to use winners' names, hometowns, and likenesses for publicity purposes without further or other compensation. Prizes won by minors will be awarded in the name of parent or legal guardian.

Participation: Sweepstakes open to residents of the United States and Canada, except for the province of Quebec. Sweepstakes sponsored by Bantam Doubleday Dell Publishing Group, Inc., (BDD), 1540 Broadway, New York, NY 10036. Versions of this sweepstakes with different graphics and prize choices will be offered in conjunction with various solicitations or promotions by different subsidiaries and divisions of BDD. Where applicable, winners will have their choice of any prize offered at level won. Employees of BDD, its divisions, subsidiaries, advertising agencies, independent judging organization, and their immediate family members are not eligible.

Canadian residents, in order to win, must first correctly answer a time limited arithmetical skill testing question. Void in Puerto Rico, Quebec and wherever prohibited or restricted by law. Subject to all federal, state, local and provincial laws and regulations. For a list of major prize winners (available after 1/29/95): send a self-addressed, stamped envelope entirely separate from your entry to: Sweepstakes Winners, P.O. Box 517, Gibbstown, NJ 08027. Requests must be received by 12/30/94. DO NOT SEND ANY OTHER CORRESPONDENCE TO THIS P.O. BOX.

The Very Best in Contemporary Women's Fiction

Sandra Brown

_____ 28951-9 TEXAS! LUCKY .... $5.99/6.99 in Canada
_____ 28990-X TEXAS! CHASE $5.99/6.99
_____ 29500-4 TEXAS! SAGE $5.99/6.99
_____ 29085-1 22 INDIGO PLACE $5.99/6.99
_____ 29783-X A WHOLE NEW LIGHT $5.99/6.99
_____ 56045-X TEMPERATURES RISING $5.99/6.99
_____ 56274-6 FANTA C $4.99/5.99
_____ 56278-9 LONG TIME COMING $4.99/5.99

Tami Hoag

_____ 29534-9 LUCKY'S LADY $4.99/5.99
_____ 29053-3 MAGIC $4.99/5.99
_____ 56050-6 SARAH'S SIN $4.50/5.50
_____ 29272-2 STILL WATERS $4.99/5.99
_____ 56160-X CRY WOLF $5.50/6.50
_____ 56161-8 DARK PARADISE $5.99/7.50

Nora Roberts

_____ 29078-9 GENUINE LIES $5.99/6.99
_____ 28578-5 PUBLIC SECRETS $5.99/6.99
_____ 26461-3 HOT ICE $5.99/6.99
_____ 26574-1 SACRED SINS $5.99/6.99
_____ 27859-2 SWEET REVENGE $5.99/6.99
_____ 27283-7 BRAZEN VIRTUE $5.99/6.99
_____ 29597-7 CARNAL INNOCENCE $5.50/6.50
_____ 29490-3 DIVINE EVIL $5.99/6.99

Deborah Smith

_____ 29107-6 MIRACLE $4.50/5.50
_____ 29092-4 FOLLOW THE SUN $4.99/5.99
_____ 28759-1 THE BELOVED WOMAN $4.50/5.50
_____ 29690-6 BLUE WILLOW $5.50/6.50
_____ 29689-2 SILK AND STONE $5.99/6.99

Theresa Weir

_____ 56092-1 LAST SUMMER $4.99/5.99
_____ 56378-5 ONE FINE DAY $4.99/5.99